FLOOD OF
MEMORIES

FLOOD OF MEMORIES

A BETH AND EVIE MYSTERY: BOOK 2

BONNIE OLDRE

gatekeeper press
Tampa, Florida

Flood of Memories

Published by Gatekeeper Press
7853 Gunn Hwy., Suite 209
Tampa, FL 33626
www.GatekeeperPress.com

Library of Congress Control Number: 2022951900

ISBN (paperback): 9781662936074
eISBN: 9781662936081

Contents

Chapter 1 1

Chapter 2 10

Chapter 3 18

Chapter 4 28

Chapter 5 34

Chapter 6 42

Chapter 7 51

Chapter 8 55

Chapter 9 64

Chapter 10 73

Chapter 11 80

Chapter 12 87

Chapter 13 96

Chapter 14 105

Chapter 15 119

Chapter 16 126

Chapter 17 133

Chapter 18 141

Chapter 19 147

Chapter 20 158

Chapter 21 166

Chapter 22 175

Chapter 23 181

Chapter 24 194

Chapter 25 204

Chapter 26 216

Chapter 27 226

Chapter 28 232

Chapter 29 242

Chapter 30 254

Chapter 31 261

Chapter 32 272

Chapter 33 280

Chapter 34 298

Chapter 1

Saturday, March 15, 1969

Beth Williams sat at the Davison City Library circulation desk and stared, in frustration, at the mostly blank pages of her notebook. She still hadn't gotten a good start on her term paper. She'd hoped to get more work done on it today. But between helping library patrons and indecision about what to write, all she had were a few scribbled notes.

After all, she thought, what could she say about *Hamlet* that hadn't already been said—and said better—by someone else? *What about the female characters? Had much been written about Gertrude or Ophelia*, she wondered. But then she envisioned the hours that she would need to spend searching through reference books and periodical indexes and sending away for obscure books and journal articles through interlibrary loans.

She shook her head no. Best to stick to a subject with easy-to-find citations. Whatever she could find at the college library, tomorrow, would have to do. She'd already asked Professor Newman for an extension on the due date, and she had to turn it in on Monday or risk getting such a bad grade that she'd have to repeat the class, which was required for her Master's in Library Science degree.

One way or another, that paper was going to get written this weekend. She'd hoped to impress him by typing it, rather than handing in a handwritten copy. But that wasn't going to happen now. If only she'd gotten an earlier start on it. She'd meant to, but time had gotten away from her.

Maybe I should write about procrastination, she thought. *That seems to be Hamlet's problem as well as mine.* She dived back in to the play. The sound of the door closing, followed by a gust of cold air, brought Beth Williams back from the gloomy ramparts of the Danish Castle, where Prince Hamlet was speaking to his father's ghost.

Beth saw Sandra Brown, whose cheeks were bright red from the cold. Winter had made a comeback, as it often did in March. Sandra rushed across the room and stopped abruptly in front of Beth, pulled off her wool hat, and blew her nose, noisily, all while staring at Beth with her eyebrows scrunched together and eyes narrowed, as though trying to remember something.

"Hello, Sandra. Can I help you with something?" Beth asked.

"Hi, Beth," Sandra said after a few moments. "No . . . That is, yes." She paused and appeared to try to gather her thoughts. "It's just that . . . I mean . . ."

"Is there a book you need?" Beth suggested.

"No, that's not it. It's about Miss Archer."

"Miss Archer?" Beth echoed. "What about her?"

Sandra leaned over the desk and dropped her voice. "You've heard . . . That is, I'm sure you must have heard, that she died."

"No! She couldn't have. I just saw her a week ago. When did this happen?"

"Last night."

Beth shook her head. "Oh no! I had no idea. It must have been sudden. Was it a heart attack or something?"

"That's just it. I don't know. This is going to sound odd, but it doesn't seem right," Sandra said.

Beth looked around to see who might be within earshot. A few kids were doing homework at a table in the children's books area. A woman stood, her back turned to the circulation desk, rifling through the card catalog.

"Let's continue this conversation in the librarian's office," Beth said. "Follow me."

Beth put the "Ring the Bell for Service" sign on the circulation desk and led Sandra through the stacks to the librarian's office. Beth left the door partly open so she could listen for the bell.

"You were saying that something doesn't seem right about Miss Archer's death?" Beth said.

"That's right. And I wondered if I could talk it over with you."

"Me? Why me?"

"Well, I understand you were Miss Archer's friend. And you solved that other case. The one about the unidentified girl."

"I wouldn't say that I solved it. I just put a few things together."

"That's not the way my dad described it. He couldn't say enough about how you put together the clues and questioned the suspects. He was very impressed."

"That was nice of him to say," Beth said, as she recalled that Sandra's dad, Mr. Brown, the banker, had been involved in that case. "But why not go to the police if you suspect something suspicious about Miss Archer's death?"

"That's just it. I wouldn't know what to say to convince them to investigate. After all, she was in her seventies and had a weak heart. Doctor Frost signed off as death by natural causes."

The bell rang at the circulation desk.

"I need to see who that is. Have a seat, won't you? I'll be back as soon as I can."

Beth hurried out to the desk. While she checked out books to a young boy, the woman who had been searching through the card catalog came over and waited to ask her a question. When it was her turn, Beth excused herself and darted back to Miss Tanner's office.

"I'm sorry," she said to Sandra. "I have another library patron waiting for help. Can we continue this conversation later?"

"Of course, I didn't mean to interfere with your job." Sandra sprang to her feet and gathered her things.

"No, that's quite all right," Beth said. "It's usually very quiet on Saturday afternoons, but you never know. Maybe we can meet later. The library closes at 5:00 p.m., so it would be a few minutes after that, if that works for you."

"That would be great. I feel so much better now, just knowing I'll be able to talk it over with you."

"Hopefully, I can help you sort it out. By the way, do you mind if my friend Evie Hanson joins us? We have plans to meet for dinner tonight. She might have some good ideas about this too."

Sandra agreed, and they decided to meet at the Big Boy restaurant. Beth closed Miss Tanner's office and followed Sandra out to the circulation desk. Sandra turned and gave her a friendly wave before leaving the library.

As Beth finished her shift, she thought back to when she last saw Miss Archer, a week ago. Beth had been planning to work on her term paper *that* weekend too, but she hadn't gotten to it. It hadn't been a normal visit, she recalled. She hadn't gotten to visit with Miss Archer, because her nephew, Melvin, had been there, and Miss Archer had seemed worried about something. Beth hadn't given it much thought at the time, assuming it had something to do with taxes, since he was an accountant.

Beth had begun delivering books to Miss Archer when she was a library volunteer in high school. Then, when she returned to her hometown, Davison City, Minnesota, twelve years after graduating from high school, and got a library assistant job, she'd volunteered to resume that task, something she'd always enjoyed.

A voracious reader, Miss Archer was in her seventies and a semi-invalid due to polio. So although she only lived a few blocks from the library, she had a hard time walking in any weather, and definitely couldn't navigate the snow and ice. Miss Archer would invite Beth in and give her tea and cookies while recounting the plots of the novels she'd finished since their last visit.

Beth would exchange the books Miss Archer had read for new ones—mostly Westerns. Miss Archer loved Zane Grey and Max Brand, and Beth brought her a half-dozen each time she visited. The library kept a tally of what she'd borrowed to avoid duplication.

Not that it mattered, Beth thought; *they were all kind of alike. There were good guys and bad guys and usually a damsel in distress who would be rescued before the end of the story. But the hero would never stick around; something kept him riding off into the sunset.*

Beth used to read Westerns, but she had graduated to mystery novels when she was in middle school and had never looked back. Still, she knew the genre, and Miss Archer's taste, well enough to pick out ones she would enjoy.

Beth recalled how she'd climbed the worn, wooden steps of Miss Archer's small, two-story house and rang the bell. While she waited, she thought, *I'll just have to explain that I don't have time to visit today.* She heard shuffling, and a small, stooped woman opened the door. She had tightly curled, white hair, and she wore slippers and a pink, crocheted sweater over a housedress.

"Oh, Beth, it's you," Miss Archer said. She peered up at Beth, her forehead wrinkled in consternation.

Beth was taken aback. Of course it was her; this was her usual day and time.

Miss Archer retreated a couple of steps to let Beth pass. "Come in. I'm sorry, but I won't be able to offer you tea today. You see, my nephew is here helping me with some paperwork."

"That's okay," Beth said. She leaned forward, while staying on the entry mat so she wouldn't track in snow, and she peeked into the small dining room. Melvin was hunched over a table strewn with folders and papers. A balding, middle-aged man, he wore an unbecoming pea-green sweater, frayed at the cuffs.

"Hi, Melvin," Beth called.

He peered up at her, over spectacles that were slipping down his nose. "Oh, yes, hello there," he mumbled, and then resumed sorting papers.

"That's fine," Beth said to Miss Archer, as she deposited the bag of books on the hall table. "I have a paper due soon, so

I'm in a bit of a rush. Unfortunately, I put it off until the last minute again."

Miss Archer smiled indulgently. "Oh good, I'm glad you understand. You're always so kind. I hope it's not too much of a bother."

"Not at all! I enjoy our visits. And I look forward to seeing you in another couple of weeks and hearing what you think of these books." She gestured toward the bag. "I also included a book on plant diseases that you wanted. Are you having trouble with your plants? African violets—aren't they? I hope not. They're so beautiful."

Beth leaned forward and studied them, arrayed behind Melvin on a plant stand in front of a south-facing window. "They do look a little droopy. Do you think they need water?" she asked.

"No." The worried expression returned to Miss Archer's face. "I water them regularly and they've always been fine, until now."

"Well, I hope you find a cure in the plant book. Speaking of books, I better take the ones you're returning and get going," Beth said.

Miss Archer shuffled off into the dining room. Beth heard her say, "Melvin, dear, where is that bag of books that was on the dining room table?"

He mumbled something in return.

"Would you please get them and give them to Beth?"

Beth heard a chair scrape across the floor, and a few moments later, Melvin appeared carrying a bag of books. He thrust it into her hands.

"Here," was all he said while avoiding eye contact. Then he turned and flounced away.

How rude! It's easy to see why he never married, Beth thought.

Miss Archer tottered back out to Beth and thanked her effusively. A few minutes later, Beth had gone home—relieved, but also a little disappointed.

As it turns out, Beth thought, returning to the present with a wave of regret, *I'll never get another chance to visit with Miss Archer.*

Chapter 2

Saturday Evening, March 15

Beth and Evie sat in a booth on the back wall of the Big Boy restaurant, which was on the outskirts of Davison City. From where they sat, they could see everyone in the place and who was coming and going. Beth checked. No one was close enough to overhear their conversation. There was only one adjacent booth, and it was vacant.

"Are we being melodramatic?" Evie asked, with a mischievous grin.

"Absolutely," Beth said. "If you ask me, Sandra is imagining things. After all, old ladies sometimes die. But there's no harm in playing undercover detectives until we know more. She should be here any minute. Thanks again for coming. I wanted to get your take on her story."

"No problem. I needed a break from studying for finals," Evie said.

Sandra came into the restaurant, stopped, looked around in a distracted way, and then, as she spotted them, raised one hand in greeting and rushed toward them.

As Beth slid over to make room, the red vinyl bench upholstery abraded her thighs in the gap between her miniskirt and the top of her nylons.

Sandra stopped abruptly when she got to their booth and stared at Evie while she pulled off her knit hat.

"I know you. Evie, right?" she said. "You used to work in the office at the sugar beet plant. According to the grapevine, you quit and went back to school."

"Yup, that's me," Evie said.

"Have a seat," Beth said, gesturing to the spot next to her.

Sandra slid in and then struggled out of her winter jacket, leaving it crumpled behind her. "Did you guys order yet?" she asked.

They said that they had.

Sandra puffed out her cheeks and slowly exhaled. "Let me get right to the point and tell you why I'm worried. Although, it's probably nothing. Tell me if you think so," she said. "Did Beth tell you what I said?" she asked Evie.

"A little bit. She said that you're concerned because Miss Archer died suddenly. Right?"

"Yeah. But there's more to it than that. It's what she said to me—" Sandra stopped, abruptly, as the waitress approached.

"Have you had a chance to look at the menu?" the waitress asked.

Sandra opened the menu and scanned it, "No, not yet. Just bring me some coffee for now."

After the waitress left, Beth prompted Sandra to continue, "What was it that you were saying? Something about what Miss Archer said?"

"Oh, yes—about a will. She said she wanted to write a new will. I tried to tell her that it could wait until she was feeling better, but she insisted that I bring her some paper and a pen."

The conversation ceased as the waitress came back with the coffee and recited the daily specials. Sandra ordered a bowl of bean soup and half a ham sandwich.

When the waitress left, Evie said, "Maybe she thought she didn't have much time left."

"That could be, but it seemed like she was improving," Sandra said. "Anyway, I brought her a pen and a pad of paper, and when I next checked on her, she was busy writing. She asked me to come back to witness her signature when she was done."

"So did you witness the new will?" Beth asked.

"No. It got busy and it was a couple of hours before I got back to check on her. When I did, she was asleep, and the writing supplies were nowhere to be seen. I assumed she put it away to think about it."

The waitress came back with their food.

"Then what happened?" Beth asked Sandra after the waitress left.

"My shift was ending, so I didn't see her again. The next day, when I came to work, I learned that she'd passed away in the night."

She paused, slowly looked from Beth to Evie with her eyebrows raised, and then said in a lowered tone, "The will was missing."

"No!" Evie said.

"Really?" Beth asked.

"Yes, really," Sandra said, as she opened the saltine packets and crumbled the crackers into her soup. "I asked the other nurses and nobody saw it. Oh, the pad of paper and the pen were there, all right, but the new will was missing."

"Do you think it might have been mislaid or discarded?" Beth asked. "If it fell on the floor while they were transferring the body, maybe the cleaner swept it up without really looking at it. Did you ask the person who cleaned the room?"

"No, I didn't. But that's a good idea. I'll find out who cleaned the room and ask them." Sandra smiled and looked much more relaxed. "I knew it was a good idea to talk to you, Beth," she said, and then took a bite of her sandwich.

"What about a visitor? Do you think a visitor might have witnessed the will for her, and then taken it with them when they left?" Evie asked.

"Not that anyone saw. I did ask about that," Sandra said.

"Could someone have slipped in and out without being observed?" Beth asked.

"Possibly," Sandra said, slowly. "The room isn't close to the nurse's station. Someone could have come up on the elevator and gone straight to her room without checking in, if they knew her room number. I'll ask the other patients down on that end of the ward if they noticed anyone visiting that night."

"Have you asked her doctor?" Beth asked.

Sandra stiffened. "No. And that's not the type of thing I'd feel comfortable asking Dr. Frost. I can't imagine him pocketing a will."

"He might have done it without thinking. What if before he examined her, he absentmindedly put it in his pocket and forgot to look at it until later?" Evie asked.

"I suppose he could have put it in the pocket of his lab coat and forgotten about it. But you know what it's like. A nurse can't ask a doctor if he made a mistake. At least I can't. It would put me on his list," Sandra said.

"His list? What list?" Beth asked.

"You know, those who warrant special attention as possible troublemakers," Sandra said.

"Got it," Beth said, as she pushed aside her empty salad bowl. "What about his lab coat? Is there any way you can check the pockets when he's not looking?"

"Maybe," Sandra said, doubtfully. "I think he leaves it in his office when he goes to lunch. Of course, I'd have to have an excuse for going into his office."

"Well, don't risk your job or anything. It's just a thought. You know, to eliminate possibilities," Beth said.

"Sure. I'll see what I can discover and let you know. When are you at the library?"

"Monday through Thursday evenings, 4:00 p.m. to 8:00 p.m., and Saturdays," Beth said.

The conversation turned to other things. Sandra asked about their classes and how Beth liked being back home in Davison City.

"I like it," Beth said. "But it's different. There's a lot more driving. For example, tomorrow I will drive to the NDSC Library and spend the afternoon working on a paper. As you know, it's about a forty-mile round trip. In the city, I used to take the bus or walk most of the time. But I'm getting used to that. And it's great to be closer to my family and reconnect with old friends." She smiled at Evie, who smiled back.

"I bet the old hometown is more exciting than you expected. I hear you guys are a real detective team," Sandra said.

Beth and Evie both assured her that wasn't true.

Beth said, "I just happened to be at the right place at the right time, or maybe you could say the wrong place and time.

Anyway, Evie and I were able to help the police piece it all together."

Sandra smiled at them, and then her smile froze, and she stared straight ahead. Beth looked in the direction Sandra was staring, but she didn't see anything out of the ordinary.

"What is it?" Beth asked.

Sandra shook her head slightly. "Nothing. I just thought of something. I have to go." She jumped to her feet and grabbed her coat. "I'll pay for my food on the way out, and I'll see you at the library in a couple of days, Beth."

"Well, that was odd," Beth said to Evie, as Sandra rushed away. "Did you see what she was staring at?"

"No. I thought I saw the door closing as if someone had just gone out, but I didn't see who it was," Evie said. "Maybe she'll fill you in next time you see her."

"What did you make of her story?" Beth asked.

"I can see why she's worried. The disappearing will is suspicious. But there's probably an innocent explanation. As you said, maybe the cleaner threw it out, the doctor pocketed it without thinking, or a visitor came and then left with it. I wonder why she wanted to change her will, though. If we knew that, it might help fill in the blanks. But I suppose there's no way to find out now."

"Unless she left some notes at home. Maybe she started to work on it before she got sick. We should go over to Miss Archer's house after we finish eating and have a look around."

"You mean, break in?"

"No, not break in. I know where she keeps an extra key. We'll just go in to water her plants and have a look around. Are you game?"

Evie grinned, nervously. "I just hope the neighbors don't call the cops."

"Why should they? They've seen me go in and out many times, so I shouldn't attract much attention."

"Unless they've heard that Miss Archer is dead. You know how quickly news spreads."

"Even so, they probably wouldn't call the cops unless I start hauling stuff out of the house. A library assistant and her friend are not exactly high-profile suspects."

"I hope you're right. Okay, I'm game," Evie said.

Chapter 3

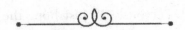

Saturday, March 15

Dusk had fallen when Beth parked across the street from Miss Archer's house. Evie pulled up and parked behind her. As Beth got out of her car, she noticed a light inside Miss Archer's living room. She ran to the driver's side window of Evie's car and tapped on it.

Evie rolled it down. "What?"

Beth put her finger up to her lips. She ran around to the passenger side and got in as quietly as she could.

"Look, someone's in the house." Beth pointed. "Turn off the car. Let's wait and see what happens."

As they watched, a shadow crossed behind the closed drapes of the living room, crossed back again, and then the light went out.

"Open your window and listen," Beth said as she cranked her window down.

Evie cranked hers down too. A few moments later, they heard the back door open and close and then the sound of a car starting.

"They went out the back," Evie said. "Should we try to follow them?"

"No, we don't know which way they're going. Stay here. Maybe they'll drive past us."

But the sound of the car receded and it fell silent.

"They didn't come this way," Evie said.

'No, they didn't. I wonder who it was. Could have been someone who just came to water the plants or something."

"Yeah, could be. I guess it wasn't a close neighbor, or they wouldn't have had to drive."

"Well, come on. The coast is clear." Beth got out of the car, and Evie followed her to the front porch.

Standing on the wooden boards of the open front porch, Beth felt under the mailbox and retrieved the little magnetic metal box that contained the front door key.

"Not exactly well hidden," Evie said.

"True. Breaking in here would not be a problem. Any number of people have used that key over the years. She has kept it there at least since I came here as a high-school library volunteer. Others have probably seen someone retrieve it, so they'd also know where it was. Security was never been a huge concern for Miss Archer." Beth inserted the key into the worn lock face, beneath the inscribed oval-shaped door handle, then returned the key to its spot.

"Do you smell that?" Beth asked as she stopped in the entryway to pull off her slush-covered boots and leave them on the rug.

As she did so, she remembered, with a pang of sorrow, that Miss Archer was no longer there to remind her not to track in snow. But whoever inherited the house certainly wouldn't want dirty floors.

Evie removed her boots too, and then sniffed the air. "Yeah. What is that, tobacco smoke? Was Miss Archer a smoker?"

"No, never. And she never let anyone smoke in her house. They had to go out on the porch. I think it must be from the previous visitor. You know how the smell of smoke clings to your clothes."

"I sure do. Remember when we sat outside Al's house in the car and watched as it burned? It took weeks to get the smell out of my things."

"Mine too. At least we solved that mystery. Unfortunately, that seems to have given some people the idea that we are a pair of super sleuths. That'll soon change," Beth said, with a laugh.

"You mean if we can't solve this one?" Evie asked.

"Yeah. If there even *is* a mystery. I'm not so sure there is. Well, we might as well investigate, since we're here. Let's start in the living room."

"What are we looking for?"

"Anything suspicious. What was the previous visitor looking for, I wonder? A will, money, or what?" Beth looked around the neat room full of overstuffed furniture with doilies tacked to the backs of seats, wondering where to start. "Last Saturday, when I dropped off Miss Archer's library books, her nephew was preparing her taxes. Maybe he left copies for her. I'll look at the desk."

Beth crossed through the living room to the small secretary desk in the back corner of the room.

Evie looked over the books on a bookshelf on the opposite side of the room. "She really liked Westerns, didn't she," Evie said as she scanned the titles.

"Um-hm," Beth replied, distracted as she opened the unlocked desk and started to root through the contents, opening small drawers and rifling through the paperwork. A ledger, containing carbon copies of checks, lay on the desk. Beth glanced through the last few pages. Nothing seemed out of the ordinary, just phone bills, utilities, payments to the drug store, and the grocery store. One caught her eye.

"Evie, take a look at this check made out to the Art Restoration and Conservation store," Beth said.

Evie came over and looked at the copy of the check. "That's interesting. I wonder what art she had that she would want to have restored."

They both looked around the room.

"Do you see anything, Beth?"

"No. Wait." Beth walked across the room and pointed to a spot on the wall next to the bookshelf. "Do you see that outline?"

Evie joined her and looked at a rectangular outline about eighteen-inches wide by twenty-four-inches long. "Yeah, it looks like something hung in that spot for a long time. The paint is darker there. The rest of the paint must have faded, but there it was protected from the sun. Do you remember what hung there?" she asked Beth.

Beth scrunched up her face, trying to visualize it. "I think it was a piece of Western art. Something like a cowboy riding into the sunset. Miss Archer never talked about it, and I guess I never looked at it too closely. We usually sat in the dining room and had tea when I visited, so I didn't see it too often. Do you think that is what she had restored?"

"Could be. I wonder how we find out."

"You could check," Beth suggested. "Maybe go over there and ask questions about art restoration. Say you're interested in it as a possible career. What do you think?"

"I don't see any harm in that," Evie agreed. "I'll check them out tomorrow. What else did you find?"

"Not much. Mostly bills." Beth sifted through the envelopes. "Wait. Here's a letter from someone."

"The envelope is yellow. It looks really old," Evie said.

"Yeah. The postmark is faded." Beth took off her glasses and held them close to her face, to get a better look with her near-sighted eyes. "What do you think?"

Beth took the letter and held it up and squinted at it. "I wish I had a magnifying glass."

Beth started to root through the drawers of the desk, looking for one. A loud knock on the door startled them. Beth shoved the paperwork back into the desk and slammed the lid. Evie was still holding the old letter. She handed it to Beth, who stuck it in her coat pocket as they crossed over to the door. Beth peered through the leaded glass inserts, let out an exasperated sigh, and opened the door.

"Hello, Officer Crample," Beth said to the large, grumpy-looking officer standing at the door. "How nice to see you."

He showed his teeth in a forced smile. "Hello, Beth. And I see that Evie is here, too. I might have guessed it was you two."

"What do you mean? What are you doing here," Beth asked.

"I'm asking the questions. What are you doing here? Trespassing?" he said.

"No, we . . . we came to water the plants," Beth stammered. "I suppose you heard that Miss Archer passed away. Suddenly. She was a friend of sorts. I always brought her library books, and I started to wonder if someone was taking care of her plants."

His head came up at the word *suddenly*, and he scrutinized Beth's face, while she avoided eye contact.

"I see. So you came here to water the plants. Have you?"

"Well, no. Not yet," Beth said.

"How long have you been here?" he asked.

"Just a few minutes," Beth said.

She followed his gaze to their boots on the door mat. The snow on them had melted into water—and then he looked back at her. "I see," he said again.

"And we were looking for the library books. So I could return them," Beth said.

"You mean those books?" Bill Crample pointed to a pile of library books on the coffee table.

Beth felt her face grow hot. To cover her embarrassment, she demanded, "You haven't said why you're here."

"I'm doing my job. Some neighbors noticed lights going off and on and called the police. But you have no business being here, so get your things and go."

"What about the plants?" Evie asked.

Bill Crample sighed loudly, stepped inside, forcing Beth and Evie to take a step back, and closed the door behind him.

"Okay, go water them then. I'll wait here. You've got five minutes." He consulted his watch. "And then you're leaving with me, even if I have to arrest you for trespassing and take you in."

"Okay, okay," Beth said. "No need to get hostile."

Beth and Evie left him standing there and went into the dining room. The African violets, lined up on a shelf by the window, were drooping. Beth felt the soil. It was damp. She looked at Evie and raised her eyebrows in surprise. Evie opened her mouth, about to say something, but Beth shook her head once. She grabbed the watering can that was sitting on the shelf next to the plants and they went into the kitchen.

After she started the water running, Beth whispered, "Quick, take a look around and see if anything looks like poison. I'll pretend to water the plants."

Evie grinned and nodded yes, and then she started quietly opening and peeking into the kitchen cupboards while Beth noisily splashed around in the sink and then carried the watering can back into the dining room. Then, keeping her back to Bill Crample, she pretended to water each of the plants.

Bill called out, "Almost done?"

"Yup, just a few more minutes," Beth replied.

She looked at Evie, who held up a canister she'd found under the sink and then quietly replaced it.

Evie went up to Beth and mouthed the words, "Rat poison."

Beth grimaced as if to say, "Yikes," and whispered, "See if you can get up to the bathroom and check the medicine cabinet before we go."

Beth put down the watering can and they went back into the hall.

"All done," Beth said. "I'll just gather those books and we'll be on our way."

"Hang on a second, I have to use the restroom," Evie said and dashed up the stairs before Bill could object.

His face reddened and he looked ready to explode. "If it was anyone else, you'd already be in the backseat of the squad car."

Beth recalled their one awful date last month, which she'd reluctantly agreed to before telling Bill that she wasn't ready to start dating again. *At least it hadn't been a total waste of time*, she thought.

"I appreciate that," she said. "By the way, we saw someone else here before we came."

"Really? Who was it?"

"I don't know, they went out the back and drove off. We didn't see them or their car."

"It's a regular Grand Central Station around here. How did you get in?" Bill asked.

"The door was open," Beth said, hoping he couldn't tell she was lying.

He scrutinized her. "Is that so? Well, it won't be open for long. Does she still keep the key under her mailbox?"

Beth looked at him in surprise. "How do you know about that?"

"It's common knowledge," he said. "So hand over the key. Or do I have to have the doors rekeyed?"

Beth reluctantly pulled the key out of her coat pocket and handed it to him while he smiled, smugly.

"I thought so," he said.

In a few moments, Evie came back downstairs, and soon they were on their way out, while Bill Crample stayed behind to make sure the house was properly locked up.

"Did you find anything in the bathroom?" Beth asked.

"Yeah, some heart medication. Maybe she did die from natural causes."

"That's possible. Can you come over to my place tomorrow afternoon to discuss what we've found so far, and what, if anything, we should do next?"

"Sure. See you then," Evie said, and they went their separate ways.

Chapter 4

Sunday Evening, March 16

Beth sat at her kitchen table with Evie and watched her taste a cookie. "What do you think?" she asked.

"Yummy. I think you've perfected oatmeal-and-chocolate-chip cookies. If your library gig doesn't work out, you could open a bakery," Evie said.

Beth laughed. "Not likely. That's a job for a morning person. Can you imagine me getting up at four in the morning?"

"No, not at all. I guess you better stick to the library. Speaking of library stuff, did you finish your term paper today? It was on *Hamlet,* right?"

"That's right," Beth said. "I finished it, and I'm turning it in tomorrow. I hope it's a passing grade. Although I probably didn't include the best sources. I kind of wish that I'd had more time to work on it. I really enjoyed rereading the play. How about your sculpture? How did that turn out?"

"It's okay. It was a fun project," Evie said.

"Meaning you'll get an *A*, I suppose."

"Only if the instructor is an easy grader."

"Such modesty. So Minnesotan of you. The fact is, you're really good," Beth said.

Evie's cheeks got red, and she waved away the compliment.

Beth put a second cookie on her plate just before Chestnut jumped up on her lap and started kneading her thighs and purring. "Don't get too comfy," she told him. "I have to get up." She plunked him down on the floor and ignored his glower while she got the coffee pot off the counter and refilled their cups.

"I read the letter we found in Miss Archer's house," Beth said. "It's very interesting. Hang on a minute and I'll get it."

Beth went to her bedroom and got the letter out of her top dresser drawer and returned to the kitchen. "I squirreled it away. No more disappearing clues, like we dealt with last time."

"Smart," Evie took a big bite out of a cookie. "Read it out loud."

Beth took the fragile, yellowed onionskin paper out of the envelope and began, "Dear Allie."

"Aw, is that Miss Archer's pet name? That's cute."

"Going on," Beth shook the letter in mock irritation. "Dear Allie, this is a very difficult letter to write."

Evie let out a small gasp, held the cookie mid-air, and stared in rapt attention.

"I will always treasure the time we spent together. But the truth is that I have met someone else."

"No! Is it a Dear John letter?" Evie asked.

Beth raised her eyebrows, nodded, and then continued reading.

I've started writing this letter a dozen different times, but couldn't go through with it. I know I should have written to you sooner, but I am a coward. I have known for several months that we could not continue our engagement. And now I have fallen in love with someone else. I didn't mean for it to happen. But it did. If I live through this war I plan to marry her, if she'll have me, and stay here in France. I am sorry if this letter causes pain. I hope that someday you will forgive me, and I wish you all the happiness in the world.

Sincerely yours,
Jack

"Wow! Poor Miss Archer," Evie said.

"I know," Beth said.

"Is there a date on the letter?"

"Yes, he wrote it on August 19, 1918."

"Wow! I have to stop saying that, but—wow! That was just a few months before the end of World War I, right?"

"That's right. It ended on November 11, 1918," Beth said.

"I wonder if Jack lived through the war and got married," Evie said.

"Yeah, I wonder that too. It's too bad that we can't ask Miss Archer." Beth realized, with a pang of sorrow, that she would never again sit at Miss Archer's dining room table with her, drinking tea and talking about books, or anything else. "Imagine, keeping that letter all these years. And she never married. It must have been quite a blow to her."

Beth checked the return address. "His name was Cooper—Jack Cooper. That's a pretty common name. I suppose it would be tough to figure out if he's still alive. Anyway, why would we? If he's still alive, he's probably forgotten all about Miss Archer."

They both sat in silence for a few moments, thinking about it.

"But it probably doesn't have anything to do with her murder, if it was a murder. Does it?" Beth asked.

"No," Evie said. "I don't see how it would connect."

"So what does that leave? You found rat poison under the sink. But if the Agatha Christie mysteries are to be believed, death from rat poisoning is pretty graphic. It wouldn't pass for a natural death. Also, she died in the hospital, not at home."

"That's true," Evie stirred a small spoonful of sugar into her coffee while thinking. "Unless whoever found her covered up the evidence."

"You mean a doctor or a nurse cleaned her up to make it look like a natural death?" Beth said. "I suppose that's possible. But then, the rat poison under her sink wouldn't have anything to do with it. Would it? I think that type of poison works pretty quickly, so if that was the poison, she would have died at home. And there are plenty of other things in hospitals to poison people."

"I guess so. The rat poison was probably just for rats," Evie said. "What about the person in the house before us? Who do you suppose that was?"

"I don't know. Maybe they came to water the plants. When I felt the soil, it was already saturated," Beth said. "I don't know how we could find out who they were or what they were doing."

"Do you suppose it was her nephew?" Evie asked.

"Could be. I could ask him. Too bad I took the library books before we left. That would have been an excellent excuse for talking to him. Now I'll have to think of some other reason."

"Maybe you could ask for tax advice. He's an accountant, right?"

"Yes, but I make so little money that my taxes are simple. He'll never believe I need to ask him about it. I'll think of something."

Evie paused to think and then said, "What about the heart medication in her bathroom? That seems to support the natural death theory."

"Yes, it could have been a natural death. In fact, it probably was. Just because we solved one murder doesn't mean that every death in town is murder."

"Right. But the disappearing will is suspicious."

"If it actually disappeared and wasn't just mislaid or carried off by someone. Sandra is supposed to let me know. So let's wait and see what she finds out. Maybe it turned up, or she will find out that someone visited Miss Archer after she started working on her new will."

"Okay. Meanwhile, we have final exams coming up this week. Are you ready for yours?"

Beth groaned. "No, I have to study for the final in my cataloging class."

"Poor you. I have a couple of exams I need to study for too. So we'd better get back at it." Evie got up and put her dishes in the sink. "Shall I help you clean up before I go?"

"Don't bother. I'll take care of it. I'll call you after I talk to Sandra, if I don't see you around campus first," Beth said.

Chapter 5

Monday, March 17

Beth walked, head down, into the library on Monday afternoon, thinking about the paper she'd handed in, hoping it was good enough. Meanwhile, thoughts about the sudden death of Miss Archer kept intruding.

When Beth arrived, the librarian, Miss Tanner, patted her red, bouffant hair and started to gather together the material she'd been working on. "It's been a quiet afternoon," she said. "Apparently, student term papers are not due yet."

"Okay," Beth, roused from her ruminations, looked around vaguely.

Miss Tanner scrutinized her. "You seem distracted, Beth. Are you okay? Miss Archer's death was a shock, I'm sure. And you just visited her recently. Didn't you?"

"Yes, and she seemed perfectly fine then. I guess you never know when your time is up."

"No, we don't know. And she was getting up in years," Miss Tanner said. She stood up, clutching selection materials and a handful of pencils. "Are you sure you're okay to work? We could close early tonight. I don't think we'd disappoint too many people."

"Oh, no. I'm fine. I just have a lot on my mind."

"Well, if you're sure. By the way, Sandra Brown is looking for you. I think she's in the periodical reading room. Why don't you go see what she wants before you take over at the desk?"

Miss Tanner headed toward her office at the back of the library, which was behind the non-fiction section. Her high heels clicked on the tile floor as she went.

Beth found Sandra flipping through the pages of the current issue of *Mademoiselle*, which featured skinny models in short skirts. She looked up and smiled. "Hi, Beth. I was passing the library, so I stopped to give you an update."

"Did you find the will?" *It would be great if it turned out that nothing sinister had happened to Miss Archer, so there was nothing to investigate,* Beth thought.

"Sorry, no. I talked to the cleaner, but he didn't find anything. I wasn't able to get into the doctor's office to check the pockets of his lab coat. But I did get some information from the patient in the room next to Miss Archer's."

"Oh? What did they say?"

"The patient, a Mrs. Schaffer, said she was awakened by a nurse taking her vitals around 10:00 p.m. on the night Miss Archer died. The nurse left the door open when she came in, so Mrs. Schaffer could see out into the hall, and she noticed a man passing by. She remembered wondering why a visitor would be there well past visiting hours. She had a thermometer in her mouth, so she didn't say anything to the nurse. A few minutes later, she saw him leave."

"Did she say anything to the nurse afterward?"

"No. I asked her that, and she said she was sleepy and didn't give it much thought until I asked her about it. One thing is, I don't know how much we can count on what she says. She's got some dementia."

"Well, if she did see someone, maybe it was a doctor or an orderly."

"Could be. She described him as a middle-aged man, balding, wearing glasses—that could be a lot of guys—except for the fact that he was wearing street clothes. She said he was wearing a jacket and boots. It's unlikely a doctor or an orderly would visit a patient in street clothes."

Beth thought a moment, and then she said, "Do you know Miss Archer's nephew, Melvin?"

"Yes, but not very well. He mostly keeps to himself," Sandra paused. "Oh, I see what you're getting at. The description fits him."

"Yeah, it does. If you get a chance tomorrow, can you ask Mrs. Schaffer if she knows Melvin and if it might have been him? Although, I suppose she probably would have said she saw Melvin if she knows him."

"Probably, but I'll check that out. And I'll try to slip into the doctor's office. It's behind the nurse's station, so it won't be easy to get into it without being noticed."

"Well, don't do anything that gets you fired. At best, it's a long shot," Beth said.

Miss Tanner appeared in the doorway, looked at Beth, then at her watch, and turned and walked away. Beth got the hint.

"Sorry, I'm needed at the desk," she told Sandra.

"Oh, sure. Sorry to keep you. I'll let you know if I learn anything new."

"Sounds good. Stop by, or call me either here or at home." She started to leave, then turned and said, "Or maybe I'll see you at the funeral, and we can talk then."

"I'll see if I can get some time off from work. I take it you're planning to go to the funeral?" Sandra said. "Has the time and date been set?"

"Not as far as I know. I suppose the obituary will be in the paper in a day or two. I'll talk to you soon." Then Beth hurried to take over for Miss Tanner.

The evening dragged on and Beth had a tough time keeping her mind on the textbook she had brought to study for the final in her cataloging class. Fortunately, it was an open-book exam, so she wasn't too worried. *It will be great to have this quarter behind me and have some free time again*, she thought.

For a few moments, she felt nostalgic for her years of living in the Twin Cities. At least then, after she returned home from work, she had time to relax and watch TV or read a book for pleasure. That is, unless she had a date with Ernie.

She grimaced at the thought. *Ah, there's the rub.* Ernie, her boyfriend of many years—Dr. Ernest Johnson—had expected full-time attention when they were together.

Mr. Flack, the town's newspaper editor, waddled up to the circulation desk. Beth looked up and smiled broadly, happy for the distraction.

"Hello, Mr. Flack. Have you finished the book on new age practices?" she asked.

"It's coming along splendidly; thank you for asking." He beamed at her. "And thank you for your help in retrieving the books I needed for my project from the NDSC library. I will have to give you an effusive mention in the acknowledgments."

"Not at all. I was happy to help," Beth wondered why he was buttering her up. "I'm just sorry you never got a chance to witness a gnostic ceremony, since the sect disbanded."

"Yes, so it would seem. Oh well. It did lead to a rather unsavory outcome." He said.

"Exactly," Beth said. "Is there anything I can help you with now?"

"As a matter of fact," he laughed in a self-deprecating fashion, "I'm putting some finishing touches on my bibliography, and I'm afraid my notes have become rather jumbled. It would be most helpful if you could double-check some citations for me.

If you have the time, that is. Of course, I would pay you for your help. As a grad student, no doubt you could use a little extra income."

"True," Beth said. "However, I'm awfully busy at the moment."

While they continued to negotiate, Beth realized that any hopes she had of a relaxing quarter break were fading away.

It would be nice to have some extra money, though, she thought. *Maybe I could pick out a few things for my apartment, or get something new to wear.* Then another idea occurred to her.

"Tell you what: I'll do it if, in addition to paying me, you write a letter of recommendation to Professor Newman, my reference class teacher, telling him how I helped you with your research. Maybe he'll give me extra credit for the experience."

"It's a deal!" Mr. Flack said. "I'll drop off my notes and a glowing letter to Professor Newman tomorrow night. Meanwhile, I'm going downstairs to take a look at some more microfilm."

"Do you need any help with that?" Beth asked.

"I don't think so, but I'll let you know." With a jaunty wave, he turned and waddled toward the staircase.

A half-hour before closing time, Beth took a break from writing overdue reminder letters and walked around the library, picking up books off of tables and reshelving them. It looked like the last few library patrons had left—no one was on the main floor. As Miss Tanner had predicted, it had turned out to be a very quiet night.

As Beth passed a table near the entrance covered with piles of tax materials, she remembered that she wanted to talk to Melvin Archer and ask him a few questions about Miss Archer. She straightened out the piles of forms on the table as she pondered how to approach him. *He'll be at his aunt's funeral,* she thought. *I'll try to talk to him afterward, at the luncheon.*

Beth went downstairs to the reference area, where she heard the whirring of microfilm being rewound, and then she remembered that Mr. Flack was still there. She found him sitting at the microfilm reader, surrounded by boxes of film and an open notebook. He was putting a reel of film back into a box.

"Did you find what you were looking for?" she asked, as she piled the microfilm reels into the return basket.

"Yes, thank you. I was just double-checking my bibliography," he said.

"Oh, good." Beth paused for a moment. "By the way, I was wondering about an obituary. I don't suppose those cross your desk."

"Sometimes. Why do you ask?"

"I was wondering about Miss Archer—a long-time library patron. I used to drop off books for her. She died on Saturday."

"Oh, I'm sorry to hear that. Yes, I did notice that one. I think her obituary will be in the paper tomorrow. She taught

English at Central High School, and I took her class. That was eons ago. Before you were born, I expect. I hadn't kept in touch, I'm afraid. I don't think she got out too much in recent years."

"No, she had some mobility issues caused by childhood polio, I think," Beth said.

"That's right! As I recall, she had a limp even as a younger woman. I'm afraid I don't remember the details of the visitation and the funeral, if that's what you wanted to know," he said.

"That's okay. I'll check tomorrow. Anyway, I just stopped by to let you know it is nearly closing time." Beth checked her watch. "In about twenty minutes."

"Okay, thanks. I'll be up shortly," he said.

As Beth finished making the rounds, she thought. *Miss Archer was a teacher. Imagine that. I knew her all those years, but I never knew that. I wonder what else I didn't know.*

Chapter 6

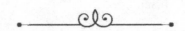

Saturday, March 22

Father McClure took the censer from the altar boy and swung it as he moved around Miss Archer's coffin, which was placed at the front of the center aisle. It clanged against its chains with a gentle rhythm while releasing clouds of sweet-smelling smoke that wafted to the back of the church where Beth and Evie sat.

Beth was surprised by the turnout. But then, funerals drew the regulars—elderly folks who marked the passing of another one of their contemporaries and congratulated themselves on outliving them. Also, as Beth had recently learned, Miss Archer had been a teacher. Many of her former students came to bid a final goodbye.

It was odd that she hadn't known that Miss Archer had been a teacher. But then, Miss Archer had rarely talked about her past. Beth had simply assumed there wasn't much to say. In all the years she had visited with her, their conversation had revolved around books, the violets Miss Archer grew, and occasionally, her nephew, Melvin.

There's probably a lot I don't know about Miss Archer, Beth thought. *Including a reason why someone might have wanted her dead.*

Father McClure finished incensing the coffin, sprinkled it with holy water as he prayed, and then headed back to the altar. Meanwhile, Beth watched the family members seated in the front pew. There were only two of them—Melvin and an elderly lady Beth hadn't met, who daubed at her eyes. Melvin sat, stiffly, apart from her.

So she probably isn't Melvin's mother. Even Melvin would be more comforting than that to his own mother, Beth thought.

There was something about the way that lady held her head that reminded her of Miss Archer.

Beth leaned toward Evie and whispered, "Do you think that's Miss Archer's sister?"

Evie shrugged.

As Beth recalled, Miss Archer had mentioned a brother and a sister. She'd said that her brother, Melvin's dad, had died in an accident when he was in his forties. She hadn't said anything about her sister. From her expression when she'd talked about her sister, Beth gathered they didn't get along. *What was her name? Something starting with a B. Was it Belinda or Bertha?*

Beth remembered thinking that Miss Archer's parents must have expected lots of children when they started naming them alphabetically, starting with Almira. Then there was her sister with the *B* name, followed by *C* for Cliff, Melvin's dad—ABC. As it turned out, they'd only had those three.

Beth skimmed the obituary printed on the back of the funeral program, looking for the names of the survivors. There it was: Mr. and Mrs. John (Beulah) Peterson. Beth grimaced at the unattractive first name. *Odd he's not here with his wife,* Beth thought. She read the preceded-in-death list. It included Miss Archer's brother, Clifford Archer, and wife. So both of Melvin's parents were deceased.

Soon the final hymn was sung and the church emptied as people headed downstairs for the funeral luncheon.

"Shall we join them for lunch?" Beth asked.

"Of course," Evie said. "Maybe we'll get a chance to ask a few questions."

As they entered the parish hall, Beth noted Melvin and his aunt, Mrs. Peterson, standing off to one side surrounded by a few people. They went over to join the group and slowly worked their way to the front.

"Hi, Melvin," Beth said. "Do you know my friend, Evie?"

He nodded stiffly, sending a light dusting of dandruff onto the collar of his worn black suit. "I think we've met," he said. He introduced them to his aunt.

Beth and Evie extended their condolences to both of them.

"Yes, it was sudden. I didn't get a chance to say goodbye. I thought we'd have more time to mend fences," Mrs. Peterson said and dabbed at her eyes with a crumpled handkerchief. "How did you know Almira?"

Beth explained how she knew Miss Archer, and asked, "So you were her only sister?"

"Yes, I am. That is, I was."

"Do you live here in Davison City?"

"No, I live in Grand Bend. We moved there after I was married. Almira stayed in the family home." She fiddled with her buttons, fastening and unfastening them. She turned to Evie.

"Were you also a library volunteer?" she asked.

"No, I didn't know her well," Evie said. "I used to see her here in church from time to time. But I hadn't seen her in some time. I gather she had mobility issues. I just came along with Beth."

Melvin had been looking over his aunt's head. Beth followed his gaze and realized that the church ladies were putting out the food and looking expectantly in their direction.

"Again, we're so sorry for your loss," Beth said.

Once out of earshot, Beth leaned toward Evie and whispered, "Mend fences! I wonder what that was all about."

They wandered around the room and stopped to chat with a few other attendees before joining the buffet line. Once they'd helped themselves to the potato and ham casserole, Jell-O salad, and a few pickles and buns, they scanned the room looking for a place to sit. The room was surprisingly full.

"There are a couple of spaces back there," Beth nodded toward the back of the room.

They made their way between the tables and chairs and took their seats. Beth hung back and let Evie choose a seat. To Beth's relief, tinged with a bit of guilt, Evie took the seat next to the garrulous newspaper editor, Mr. Flack. Beth sat down next to her.

On Beth's left was an elderly lady whom she hadn't met. Once they were settled, they introduced themselves. She said her name was Mrs. Wren.

"Were you a friend of Miss Archer's?" Beth asked.

Mrs. Wren cupped her ear. "What did you say?"

There was a lot of background noise, as everyone talked at once. Beth raised her voice and repeated the question.

"Oh yes, I've known her for years. We're both members of the African Violet Society. That is to say, she *was* a member," Mrs. Wren said.

"I'm afraid her violets aren't in very good shape," Beth said. "It looks like they've been overwatered, or underwatered, or something. I don't know much about them."

"Oh dear!" Mrs. Wren looked shocked. "Almira would not be happy about that."

"I guess not. I don't suppose you'd like to take them and nurse them back to health?" Beth said.

"No, I'm afraid not," Mrs. Wren said. She seemed quite flustered by the suggestion. "I'm sure Mr. Wren would never allow it." She glanced in the direction of the timid-looking man, seated to her left, who seemed oblivious to the whole conversation. "I have far too many as it is. Also, one would hate to perhaps introduce a diseased plant and end up losing them all. No, that wouldn't do."

Beth decided to try to introduce a safer subject. "I was surprised to learn that Miss Archer was a teacher. She never mentioned it in all the years I knew her."

"Indeed?" Mrs. Wren raised her thin eyebrows and gazed at Beth. "You seem very young to have known Almira for many years."

"Well, I started bringing her books from the library when I was in high school—as a volunteer," Beth said.

"Oh! So you're Beth Williams. I hadn't quite placed the name. Oh yes. Almira mentioned you often. She seemed very fond of you, and she enjoyed your visits."

Beth felt the heat rising in her cheeks and waved away the compliment. "It was my pleasure. Miss Archer was always so interested in the books I brought her, and she loved to talk about them. But as I said, she never mentioned being a teacher."

"That is perfectly understandable after what happened," Mrs. Wren said.

"Why? What happened?" Beth asked.

"She was unjustly fired!"

A loud harrumph from the other side of the table interrupted their conversation. Beth looked up to see a heavily made-up woman with tightly curled hair glaring at them. "I don't think this is the time to be getting into all that!" she said.

A moment of silence descended on their side of the table. Mrs. Wren's face fell and she started to blink rapidly. She stared down at her plate. The angry woman looked away and, with a forced smile, continued a conversation with the person seated next to her.

Mrs. Wren turned away from Beth and started talking to her husband. A few minutes later, she said goodbye, and they left.

Beth turned toward Evie, who was being regaled by Mr. Flack about his book.

"Who's that?" Beth muttered, nodding slightly toward the woman across the table from her.

Evie wrinkled her brow in thought. "I'm not sure," she whispered.

Mr. Flack said, "Then the publisher told me to cut that chapter. But it is integral . . ." he trailed off, noticing that he'd lost his audience.

He nodded to the woman across the table who had scolded Mrs. Wren, then shifted his gaze to Evie and Beth, raised his eyebrows, and launched back into his chapter-by-chapter book description. A few moments later, the angry woman and her husband also left.

Mr. Flack leaned toward Beth and Evie and asked, "What did I miss?"

"I'm not sure," Beth said. "The woman who was there," she pointed, "got angry at something that Mrs. Wren, who was sitting there, said."

"What did Mrs. Wren say?" he asked.

"That Miss Archer was unjustly fired from her teaching job," Beth said.

"Ah, well, I wouldn't say fired. More like encouraged to resign, I believe. Let's see, that would have happened before your time. It was all kept pretty hush-hush, as I recall. Do you know any of the details?" he asked Evie.

"No, I don't think so. When was this?" Evie said.

"It must have been the late 1940s," he said. "Naturally, as a former student, it was on my radar. There was some sort of cheating scandal, followed by expulsions, and then Miss Archer left."

"Do you know the woman who got so angry?" Beth asked Mr. Flack.

"Yes, that was Mrs. Selvig. Her daughter was one of the students who were expelled due to cheating."

"Interesting," Beth said.

Mr. Flack glanced around, seeing to check if anyone was eavesdropping on their conversation. Several heads had turned in their direction.

"Let's continue this conversation another time," he said.

Then he returned to his favorite subject—his book. Beth and Evie soon excused themselves and made a hasty exit.

Chapter 7

Sunday, March 23

Beth was in the kitchen at her parent's house, helping prepare the family's Sunday dinner. She peeled the potatoes and carrots and dropped them into a bowl of salted water to be added, later, to the pot roast. Meanwhile, her mother seasoned the beef roast and dredged it in flour. As they worked, Beth told her about Miss Archer's funeral.

"Mom, do you remember a cheating scandal at Central High in the late forties?" Beth asked.

"Oh, yes, I do remember that. They tried to keep it hushed up, of course, but I think everyone knew about it. It's hard to keep a secret in this town. What brings that up?"

Beth told her about Mrs. Selvig and her reaction to the comment that Miss Archer had been fired from her teaching job.

"That's not surprising," Mom said, as she speared the roast with a large fork and lowered it into the sizzling fat into the roasting pan. "Her daughter, Anna—I think that's her name—was one of the girls who was expelled."

"Did you know her?"

"A bit, but not well; she was a lot younger than me," Mom said, as she checked the roast to see how it was browning. "And her family was kind of stand-offish. I assumed it was because they were an old family and we weren't."

"An old family?"

"Yes, her family was one of the first to settle in Davison City. But maybe it was more than that."

"Why, what do you mean?" Beth discarded the peelings, then rinsed and dried her hands.

"I shouldn't say, because I don't know for sure . . ."

"You don't know what?" Cathy, Beth's sixteen-year-old sister, poked her head into the kitchen. She'd just come up from the downstairs family room. The sound of the TV traveled up behind her and then muted when she shut the door.

"Never mind," Mom said. "I suppose Dad is asleep?"

"Yup, there's nothing on TV, so I came upstairs. What are you guys talking about?" Cathy sniffed the lemon meringue pie sitting on a cooling rack on the counter.

"Beth was telling me about Miss Archer's funeral from yesterday. It sounds like she had a good turnout."

"Oh, fun." Cathy made a face, then asked her mom. "Are Gary and Debbie coming for dinner?"

"Yes, but they won't be here for a while yet. I think they're painting the baby's room this afternoon," Mom said.

"Oh no, working on a Sunday," Cathy said, in mock horror.

"I know. I wish your brother could take the whole day off," Mom said. "But he's working at the garage six days a week, so Sundays are the only days he can get things done around his house. Speaking of work, have you done your homework?"

"Mom! I was just going," Cathy said. Then, with some eye-rolling and complaining, she stomped out of the kitchen.

"How about you, Beth? How's school going for you?"

"Okay, I guess. I finished winter quarter, so I have a few days off before spring quarter starts on Wednesday."

"Great! Are you doing anything fun?"

Beth snorted. "I wish! No, I'm helping Mr. Flack, the newspaper editor, with some library work for the book he's writing. So I'm busier than ever. I've been in the college library during the day and at my library job in the evenings."

"Is Mr. Flack paying you?"

"Yup, that's the good part. Also, I wrangled a letter of recommendation out of him to give to my reference professor. Which, hopefully, will get me an *A* in his class. Anyway, what was it you were saying about Anna Selvig?"

"Oh, right," Mom added a little beef broth and a bay leaf to the pan, covered it, and adjusted the burner to low. "Just that she was never the same after she was expelled. She started running with a wild crowd and then dropped off the map. I haven't heard a thing about her in years. She could be perfectly fine, of course. I just don't know."

Soon, Gary and Debbie showed up, and the conversation turned to painting the nursery and getting ready for the baby.

Chapter 8

Monday, March 24

Beth's rumbling stomach reminded her it was past lunchtime. Normally, she and Evie met in the cafeteria for lunch. But it was quarter break. Evie was at home, and the cafeteria was only open for a couple of hours for lunch each day. Checking her watch, Beth realized she'd missed the window. She'd have to head off campus to find a nearby café. But first, she decided, she would check one more citation.

She picked out one of the 3x5 cards that she'd used to organize Mr. Flack's citations and started down the stacks of the NDSC's library, searching for *Prominent People of Davison City*. She'd verified the publication information from the card catalog, but to double-check the quotations and page numbers, she'd have to retrieve the book. It was located in the 977s, way back in the dusty corner of the top floor of the library, where they kept the older books with Dewey Decimal Classification numbers (DDC). The library had since switched over to the Library of Congress classification (LCC).

Beth found the book. It was on a top shelf, of course. She stood on her tiptoes and stretched. But at five-foot-four inches tall, she still couldn't reach it. So she rounded up a rolling step stool, kicked it over, climbed upon it, and retrieved the book.

Beth took it to a nearby table, sat down, and quickly checked the page citations—all correct. On an impulse, she searched the index for Selvig. Sure enough, the name appeared in several places in the book. She flipped to the first page indicated and read about Mr. Ole Selvig, an immigrant from Norway. He had purchased some railroad land when it was first offered for only one dollar an acre. That land was later incorporated into Davison City.

So the Selvigs were, indeed, some of the earliest settlers to Davison City, and the sale of their farmland as city lots was the source of their wealth. According to the brief biography, at the time they came, they faced an empty wilderness on the outskirts of civilization with hordes of mosquitoes in the summer, spring floods, and viciously cold winters. Which explained why no one had ever settled there permanently. Although, Native Americans had hunted there when it wasn't flooded or covered by snowdrifts. The Selvigs had stayed and eventually prospered, while many other settlers gave up and left.

Well, good for them, Beth thought. She closed the book and placed it on a reshelving cart while wondering what had become of Anna Selvig. *Where was she? Was she still nursing a grudge against Miss Archer for the part she'd played in her expulsion from high school? Had Anna come back to seek revenge?*

There were so many questions. Beth wondered if Mr. Flack might know. He'd seemed to imply that he did when they'd met at the funeral luncheon. She decided to ask him about it if he checked in at the library tonight, as expected, to see how she was doing on his project.

I really should track down something to eat, Beth thought after another tummy rumble as she shuffled through the 3x5 index cards of citations she still needed to verify. But there were only a few more to go. She decided to stick with it and finish up. Then she'd have part of the day off before work tomorrow. It would be great to be able to sleep in, get a few chores done, and even spend a little time with her pet cat. *Poor Chestnut; he must be lonely,* she thought.

Beth dug through her purse and fished out a half-roll of LifeSavers. *This will tide me over,* she thought as she popped one into her mouth.

Beth flew into the Davison City Library just as the clock struck four.

As usual, Miss Tanner looked at the clock on the wall, over the top of her reading glasses, before looking at Beth and smiling. "Good afternoon, Beth," she said. "I have some news."

Beth paused, as she was just about to rush past the circulation desk to hang up her things in the librarian's office. Miss Tanner was smiling. That was a good sign.

"Oh? What news is that?" Beth asked.

"Go ahead and put away your things. It will keep," Miss Tanner said, with a mysterious smile.

Beth quickly hung her wraps on the coatrack in the corner of the office, kicked off her boots, and put on her shoes. She did a quick check in the small wall mirror. Her light-brown, shoulder-length hair looked fairly neat for a change. Only her bangs stuck up from static electricity. She licked her fingers and patted them smooth over her hazel eyes and cheeks that were still pink from the cold, adjusted the wide, paisley print headband, and hurried out for her shift.

Miss Tanner had piled up her books and papers and was tapping a pencil on the desk when Beth joined her. She looked Beth over, seeming to approve of her pantsuit. Beth had convinced Miss Tanner that, at least during the colder months of the year, pants were appropriate workwear. A more formal person, Miss Tanner continued to wear her Chanel-inspired tweed suits and skirts, nylons, and high heels.

"We have a bequest," Miss Tanner said.

"A bequest?" Beth echoed.

Miss Tanner looked annoyed. She took off her reading glasses, which were attached to a beaded chain, and let them fall on her chest.

"Yes, a bequest. I know you have a lot on your mind, but try to focus!" She held up a letter.

"When you say, 'We have a bequest,' do you mean the library?"

"Obviously," Miss Tanner said. "Miss Archer left us something in her will. The library has inherited her books."

"Her will? Which will?"

"Which will?" Miss Tanner looked incredulous. "Miss Archer's will. Do try to keep up, dear. She left us her book collection. Her solicitor sent us a letter to that effect."

"I see. Yes, of course."

Beth wondered if she should say anything about the will Miss Archer was writing in the hospital.

"I thought you'd be pleased," Miss Tanner said.

"I am. It was just unexpected. Doesn't her family want her books?"

"I don't know about that. Perhaps the books are not their type of literature, or not of great monetary value, and Miss Archer just wanted to be sure they weren't discarded without a look."

"I suppose that could be. As I recall, they were mostly Westerns, a mixture of hardbacks and paperbacks, with a few older books that might have been classics," Beth said.

"Are you busy tomorrow?" Miss Tanner asked.

Beth's heart sank as she realized her hopes for a partial day off were evaporating. "No, I guess not."

"I was wondering if you could go over there and start packing up the books. I can arrange for someone to haul them over to the library once that's done. I believe you have one more day of spring break before your classes start. It would mean additional pay, of course."

Beth thought for a moment. "Would it be okay to bring a friend along?"

"You mean Evie, the nice young lady who helped us out at our last library fundraiser? I suppose that would be all right. But I don't know if I could arrange to pay her. I would have to run that past the Library Board, and they are not always as generous as we might wish."

"Oh, that's okay. It's not that big of a job. I'm sure she'd be happy to help if she's free," Beth said, thinking that she might have to promise Evie pizza and cookies in return for her help.

"Mr. Nobis has the key. He said you could swing by and pick it up from his secretary. There are boxes downstairs in the workroom. So what do you say—are you willing?"

Beth agreed, and they discussed the details. Later, she called Evie, who said she'd come over to Beth's apartment the next morning at around nine o'clock.

At least I can sleep in for an hour or two. The chores will have to wait until the weekend, Beth thought.

Later that evening, Mr. Flack leaned on the Davison City Library's circulation desk, checking the pages of citations that Beth had given him. She had noted a few minor corrections.

"Good work, Beth. Of course, I was sure it would be, so I prepared the letter of recommendation you requested. You can read it and, if it is satisfactory, send it to your professor." He handed her a business-sized envelope. "I also enclosed a check for the agreed amount, so be sure to remove that before you seal it."

"Thank you, Mr. Flack. It was a good experience," Beth said. "It was also interesting. In fact, today I was looking at one of the books on your list, the one about the Davison City settlers, and I came across some information about the Selvig family. I learned that they were one of the first families to settle here."

"Oh, yes, that's true. That was in the 1850s, if I remember correctly. That isn't the focus of my current research, so I could be wrong . . ."

Beth let him rattle on, while she smiled and nodded, waiting for a chance to ask about Anna. When he finally paused for a breath, she interjected, "So I suppose Anna is about the third generation American-born?"

"Let me think." He held up one hand and counted off with the fingers of the other hand. "First there was Ole, the Norwegian immigrant, and then his son, that would have been Anna's grandfather. But I don't know if he was born in Norway, or here. And then her father, he was born here, of course, and then Anna and her brother, Sven. So I guess that would make the kids second- or third-generation Americans, depending on where their grandfather was born."

"Anna has a brother?"

"Oh, yes. Sven Selvig. He moved to the cities for college and rarely comes home."

"Oh, that's too bad. I understand that Anna has disappeared. Is that right? That must be tough on the parents with both kids pretty much out of the picture."

"I suppose so, though they don't talk about it. But yes, Anna left home shortly after the cheating scandal and hasn't been back, as far as I know. I don't know the Selvigs well, so I couldn't say for sure."

"What do you recall about the scandal? What happened, and how was Miss Archer involved?" Beth asked.

"It was hushed up, as you can well imagine, since Mr. Selvig was on the town council at the time, and he prides himself as being a member of a founding family," Mr. Flack said. "I think the kids were paying someone to write their term papers. Miss Archer noted the similarity in style, and the difference between assignments done in class and those done outside of class. And she called it to the attention of the principal."

"And that led to expulsions and Miss Archer leaving teaching? That seems like an overreaction."

"Well, yes, but it snowballed," Mr. Flack said. "Initially, the students were given a chance to rewrite their papers for a reduced grade, and most of them did. But Mrs. Selvig was adamant that her daughter hadn't cheated. She made such a stink about it that the school had to investigate. And when they did, they found that Anna had, indeed, cheated. Not just once, but repeatedly. Apparently, she was one of the ring leaders in the scheme and was taking kickbacks from the fees the kids were paying for their plagiarized papers. So the school was forced to expel her."

"But why did Miss Archer have to retire?"

"Mr. Selvig got involved. He put pressure on the school to encourage Miss Archer to take an early retirement. There was some sort of vague threat of withholding funds, I believe. Although, I doubt he had the authority to do so."

"And then Anna took off for parts unknown?"

"Not immediately. She left after her father lost his seat on the city council in the next election," Mr. Flack said.

Beth paused a moment to digest this information. "Her mom and dad must have blamed her and made things unbearable for her."

"Yes, that's likely. Mr. Selvig never again ran for elected office, and he became somewhat reclusive."

"What a tragedy! I bet the Selvigs were not big fans of Miss Archer." Beth thought for a moment. "But then, I wonder why they showed up at her funeral."

"Good question. To make sure she was dead, perhaps," Mr. Flack said, and then chuckled. He soon segued back to talking about his book, until Beth told him it was time to get ready to close for the night.

As she checked the library and warned people it was nearly closing time, she pondered Mr. Flack's statement, and a thought crept into her mind. *Did the Selvigs do something to ensure that Miss Archer was dead?*

Chapter 9

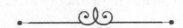

Tuesday, March 25

Beth and Evie parked in the back of Miss Archer's house and let themselves in through the back door, into the kitchen. The first thing they did was stop and check the container of rat poison under the sink. It looked like it hadn't been touched.

Anyway, Beth thought, *it was unlikely this was what poisoned Miss Archer.* She'd been reading up on poisons, and the symptoms of rat poison would be hard to misdiagnose as a heart attack.

Beth said, "Didn't she have some heart medication in the bathroom? What was it?"

"Yeah, But I can't say for sure what it was. I just took a quick look."

"Let's check," Beth said.

On their way through the dining room, Evie paused and pointed at the African violets, drooping over the edges of their pots. "Boy, those sure don't look healthy. Do you think they need water?"

Beth felt the soil in each pot. "No, the soil is still damp. Same as it was the last time we were here. If anything, I'd say they've been overwatered. You know what that means?"

"No, what?" Evie asked.

"Someone else has been in the house since we were last here. Otherwise, these plants would have dried out by now."

They looked wide-eyed at each other. "Do you think it was a neighbor, the nephew, or maybe the sister?" Evie asked.

"Could be anybody. Maybe more than one person. If a couple of people are both watering the plants that would account for the overwatering. Who knows how many people have a key to this place?" Beth said.

They went through the dining room and started up the stairs, which were opposite the front door. Beth held her breath as they crept upstairs, listening for the sound of someone else in the house, but all she heard was her breathing and an occasional creaking of the steps.

Once in the bathroom, Evie opened the medicine cabinet and then stopped and stared. "I thought it was right here." She pointed to an empty spot on the bottom shelf.

"Are you sure?"

"No, I'm not sure. I was in a hurry. But I *think* so. That's weird." Evie moved the bottles and boxes around. But there weren't any prescription medicines, just aspirin, antacids, and the like. "Do you suppose someone took it?"

"Who? The killer, because it was tampered with, you mean? This is starting to look pretty suspicious." A chill ran down Beth's spine. "Come on, let's go downstairs, box up those books, and get the heck out of here. I don't want anyone to find us snooping around."

They went down to the study and started to assemble boxes, unfolding and taping them.

Something caught Beth's eye, so she straightened up and pointed to the painting on the wall next to the bookshelf. "Look! Wasn't that missing before?"

Evie stopped, walked up to the painting, and examined it. "Yeah. That definitely wasn't here before. So I guess the art restoration people must have returned it. But that's weird. How did they get in?"

"It *is* weird, isn't it?" Beth said. "Do you suppose Miss Archer gave them a key? Or did a neighbor or Miss Archer's nephew let them in?"

Beth and Evie examined the painting. A cowboy on horseback sat on a rock outcropping and stared at the setting sun. The sunset was rendered in bold oranges and reds against a deep blue sky that contrasted with the white of the snowcapped mountain.

"What do you think of it?" Beth asked.

"I like it. I think it's a Charles Marion Russell." Evie examined the signature.

"Is it valuable?"

"I'm no expert, but it could be. I'll try to find out more about him."

"I guess it's another puzzle piece to ponder. Meanwhile, we'd better get these books packed up."

They finished assembling a few more boxes and then started packing from the bottom shelf of the bookcase, working their way up. To get to the top shelf, Beth hauled a heavy wooden chair out of the dining room and climbed up on it. She grabbed handfuls of paperback books off of the top shelf and passed them down to Evie, who packed them into the box at her feet.

"I feel kind of weird doing this," Beth said. "Like Miss Archer is going to step into the room and ask us what on earth we think we're doing."

"I bet. After all the time you spent with her, it must be hard to think that she's never coming back," Evie packed the books into the box, following Beth's advice to fill the box evenly, so they wouldn't shift when moved.

Beth paused and glanced at the spines of the books. "It's kind of sad to think of how she carefully selected and kept all of these books, and now they aren't worth much. The library already has a lot of these titles. Most of these will probably end up in the white elephant book sale."

"Yeah, but as a fellow book lover, Miss Archer obviously wanted to give them to you so they would go to another book lover. If someone buys one for a quarter, at least it gets one more read."

"True. Well, that's it for the top shelf," Beth was about to climb down when she spotted a box on top of the bookcase, pushed to the back wall. "Hang on. There's a box up here." She stood on her tiptoes and tried to grab it. "It's too far back. I can't get it."

"Let me try," Evie said. "I'm at least six inches taller than you."

They exchanged places, and Evie pulled the box toward her, grabbed it with both hands, and slowly lowered it down to Beth. "Wow, this is heavy."

"No kidding," Beth said, as she took it. "It weighs a ton! What do you think is in it?"

"Gold bars? Bricks? Let's see." Evie hopped off the chair, and then Beth put the box on it. The top was covered with a thick layer of dust, and the box was tied shut. Beth tried, without success, to untie the string.

"Here, let me try," Evie said. She struggled with it for a few more minutes. "Nope, not gonna work. We need a knife."

"I'll get one." Beth went to the kitchen, rooted around in drawers, and returned in a few minutes with a paring knife. "This should do the trick."

Evie cut the string and lifted open the flaps. Inside was some tissue paper, which she removed. Underneath that were leather-bound books with gold etching around the edges of the covers, but no front titles.

"Wow, look at these!" Beth picked one up. The spine was richly adorned with gold etching, and on three lines, it read SHAKE- SPEAR'S WORKS.

Beth gasped. "I wonder. Could it be?"

"Could it be what?" Evie asked.

"Come on. Let's take it into the dining room, where we can get a better look at it." Beth placed the volume back into the box, carried it into the dining room, put it on the table, and switched on the overhead light. Then she gingerly removed one of the volumes and carefully opened it to the title page, and gasped again.

"What is it? You're scaring me," Evie said.

"This might be a first edition of Shakespeare's collected works. I just read about these while I was doing my paper on *Hamlet*. Look at this."

Beth and Evie bent over the book.

"See?" Beth pointed to the title page and read it out loud, "*The Works of Mr. William Shakespeare; in Six Volumes.* By N. ROWE, Esq; London: Printed for Jacob Tomson, within Grays-Inn Gate, next Grays-Inn Lane. MDCCIX."

"MDCCIX, what's that?" Evie asked.

"That's the date in Roman numerals. That means . . ." Evie paused and thought a moment. "That's 1709, I think."

"So that means that these books are . . ." Evie stopped and counted on her fingers. "Two hundred and sixty years old. Is that right?"

"Yeah, if they're real—which seems unlikely," Beth said. "If they're genuine, they are very valuable. How would Miss Archer ever have been able to afford them on a teacher's salary? Maybe they're reproductions."

"Yeah, maybe," Evie sounded disappointed.

Beth pulled the six volumes out of the box and piled them on the table. At the bottom of the box was an envelope. "Hey, look at this."

On the outside of the envelope, in cursive script, it read, "To Almira." Beth opened the envelope and pulled out an old-fashioned frilly Valentine's Day card, yellowed with age. The outside of the card was adorned with a small bouquet between two hearts and read, "Love's Message to my Valentine." The printed message inside the card read, "A Heart's Gift." Underneath was a handwritten note. "I thought of you when I found these in an antiquarian bookstore in London. I knew that as an English major, you would appreciate them. I hope you will accept these books as a token of my love." It was signed, "Jack."

"Boy, what a gift! He must have really loved her," Evie said. "And then he dumped her. I wonder what happened to change his mind."

A loud knock on the back door made both of them jump. Beth hurriedly put the books back into the box, put the card and envelope on top of it, and closed it.

"That's probably just the library janitor," Beth said.

She went to the back door and peered through the curtain on the window, and saw John Thompson standing there, staring back at her. She let him in.

"Hi, John. Here to pick up the books?"

"Yes, ma'am. I brought my hand truck." He gestured toward the battered red two-wheeler next to him. "Where are the books?"

"Through the living room, into the study."

He trudged through the kitchen and dining room. Beth noted with dismay the dirty slush he was tracking across the floor from his rubber boots and the wheels of the hand truck that he dragged behind him.

A fleeting thought crossed her mind. *Miss Archer would be mad.* Then she remembered, with a sinking feeling, that Miss Archer wasn't around to mind anymore. *Still, there's no reason to leave the place in a mess. I'll wipe up the tracks before we leave.*

John came back through the dining room with four boxes stacked precariously on the cart.

"Want I should take that one too?" he asked, as he headed toward the box on the table.

Beth stepped in front of it. "No. That's okay. I'll take that one."

He shrugged and mumbled something. When one of the boxes toppled off the hand truck, as he dragged it across the threshold, Beth was glad she hadn't added her box to the top of the pile.

Miss Tanner was suitably impressed when Beth brought in the box of Shakespeare books when she arrived for work that evening. Like Beth, she wasn't sure if they were genuine.

"I'll have an expert authenticate them. But until I can get down to the Cities, I'll keep them locked up at home. Meanwhile, mum's the word," she said.

Beth promised she and Evie would keep them secret.

Chapter 10

Wednesday, March 26

For lunchtime, the cafeteria was not very crowded. Since today was the first day of the spring quarter, Beth guessed that a lot of students were still finding their way around campus. With a choice of open tables, Beth and Evie picked one next to the outside glass wall, where they could watch icicles drip in the sun.

Evie said, "Thanks for lunch, and for doing the driving today."

"No problem. It's the least I could do after all your help boxing up books. I'm just glad that our schedules work out, so we can take turns driving this quarter. No point for both of us making the forty-mile round trip if we don't have to," Beth said.

"That's true." Evie smiled. "But as I recall, there was also an offer of pizza for helping with those books. Remember?"

"I remember." Beth paused. "Say—what if we make it a fish fry instead?"

"Even better. I'm in. Where and when?"

"I was thinking of the church's Friday fish fry. It's pretty popular. A lot of the people go. Maybe we'll get a chance to ask a few questions."

"Like what?"

"Like about the Valentine's Day card." Beth patted her purse. "I have it here. I was about to bring the box into the library when I remembered it. Since it's not a book, I figured it didn't belong to the library. So I took it out of the box and put it into my purse. But now I'm not sure who to give it to. Do you think Miss Archer's sister might want it?"

"Maybe. But she probably won't be at the fish fry, since she lives here in Grand Bend, not in Davison City," Evie said. "By the way, what did Miss Tanner think of those old Shakespeare books?"

"Pretty much the same as us. She didn't want to get too excited until she can get them authenticated. That reminds me. She wants us to keep mum about it."

Evie shrugged, "Okay. But why?"

"I'm not sure." Beth poked at her salad in a small, faux-wood salad bowl, which she'd drenched with two pumps from the French dressing dispenser and topped with a generous scoop of croutons. "I suppose she's worried that someone might break into her house and steal them. She took the box home with her to keep it until she can get them to the Cities to be appraised."

Evie snorted. "Steal them! They sat in Miss Archer's house undisturbed for over fifty years, so I'm guessing theft of rare books is not a huge problem around here."

"Sure. But maybe no one knew about them. I sure didn't. I suppose she might also be concerned about funding. Rumor has it the city council is threatening to cut our budget. If they think we have a valuable asset, that might give them an excuse for doing that. And then, if the books turned out to be reproductions, the library would be left in the lurch. That could result in cutting my position."

"They wouldn't do that. Would they? The town would be up in arms if the library had to reduce its hours," Evie said.

"I hope you're right," Beth said. "Otherwise, I might end up going back to work for Ma Bell, like I did for eight years in the Cities."

"You don't want to do that! You hated it."

"I did. When I took the job, I didn't think of it as long-term. Just something to do for a year or two, until I got married. Big mistake!"

"Do you ever hear from Ernie?"

"Nope. Unless you count reading about his engagement in the Society Pages."

"Already? He didn't waste any time, did he?"

"Not once he found a rich girl whose daddy would pay off his medical school loans—just guessing. But I don't want to talk about him. Have you heard from Jim lately?"

"Yeah. There's no phone where he is now, so no phone calls. But he writes to me. Sometimes there's a delay. Some weeks I get no letters from him, and then I get a few at a time. I got a couple of letters last week."

"Is he in a dangerous place in Vietnam?"

"He can't say exactly where he is. He tries to make it sound like a big adventure, like an extended camping trip. I won't know how he really is until he gets home." Evie wrinkled her brow and stirred her soda with the straw. She looked up and forced a smile. "Meanwhile, I guess we're both just a couple of old maids. I think we waited too long to get married. Most of our friends from high school are married and already have kids."

They stared out the window at the melting snow for a minute.

"No way! Times are changing," Beth said. "Thirty is the new twenty." She was happy to see this assertion made Evie smile, if a bit skeptically. "Anyway—back to the Friday fish fry. Do you think that we should ask Melvin about the card, if he's there?"

Evie considered the idea. "I don't think so. He's unlikely to know or care about a card from Miss Archer's long-lost boyfriend. What about that friend we spoke to at the funeral?"

"You mean the African violet lady? What was her name?"

"Mrs. Wren," Evie said.

"That's right, Mrs. Wren. I wish I had your memory for names. She must be about Miss Archer's age. I probably won't ask her about the card, but we could see if she remembers anything about Jack. And we could ask Miss Archer's sister, Beulah Peterson. We could stop and see her this afternoon if she's home. If that's okay."

"Yup, works for me," Evie said.

After lunch, Beth called Mrs. Peterson from a payphone and arranged the visit. Then they went their separate ways.

Beth had some time between her last class and meeting Evie, so she went to the library and retrieved the *Prominent People of Davison City*. Browsing through it, she noted that the town had been founded in 1872. Miss Archer was born in 1895. Maybe her family was among the early settlers, like the Selvigs. She wondered what other first families might have known Miss Archer when she was a girl, and knew secrets that could provide a motive for murder.

Beth remembered Miss Archer talking about how the city streets were unpaved when she was a girl. Beth wished she'd paid more attention to her stories. If she had, Miss Archer might have shared more of them.

Beth checked out the book and took it with her. She had just settled into a beanbag chair in the student union and opened the book when Evie walked up.

"Done already?" Beth said as she struggled out of the chair.

"Yup. The instructor just took attendance, handed out the syllabus, and gave us our first assignment. Ready to go?" Evie said.

"I guess so. If you'd gotten here any sooner, I wouldn't have been back from the library. Look what I took out." Beth held up the book.

"Checking more citations? I thought you were done with that project."

"I am. This is for the case. I thought we should know more about Miss Archer. We can look for names of early settler families and see if anything jumps out."

"Jumps out how?"

"As someone to talk to for background information," Beth said. "Miss Archer's sister won't expect us for another forty-five minutes. Want to hang out here, or stop somewhere for a coffee?"

"Let's hang out here. I'm still pretty well caffeinated. But let's find a table. I'm not sure I want to sit in one of those." Evie pointed to the beanbag chair.

Beth laughed. "Good choice."

They sat at a nearby table and browsed through the library book until it was time to go. Evie identified several names of the early settler families whose descendants still lived in Davison City.

Beth said, "It's a big help that you know so many people."

"I guess there's something to be said for staying in one place," Evie said.

They packed up their things and headed out.

Chapter 11

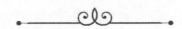

Wednesday, March 26

Beth drove slowly down the street while peering at house numbers. The Petersons' house was in the new subdivision on the outskirts of Grand Bend. Once she had located it, Beth saw it was a ranch-style house, nearly identical to the others on the block, distinguished only by its color—a pinkish-beige. The surrounding houses were white or gray.

Mrs. Peterson, a tall woman with tightly curled, iron-gray hair, came to the door and led them into the beige-and-white interior of her house. First, she directed them to take off their boots before leading them into the adjacent dining space, which was partially separated from the large, galley-style kitchen by an island. Then she sat down, erectly, in one of the dining room chairs and invited them to join her.

Beth and Evie struggled out of their winter jackets and hung them on the backs of their chairs before sitting down. Beth heard the muffled sound of a television from somewhere in the house. Presumably, Mr. Peterson was watching it.

Beth noted the modern surroundings. The dining set had spindly, tapering legs. It was an attractive if somewhat sterile room, almost a polar opposite to her late sister's cozy house. Overall, it seemed like the Petersons were pretty well-off. Beth guessed they must be retired and had probably recently moved into this new, one-story house in anticipation of future mobility needs.

Mrs. Peterson poured coffee from a white carafe into white-and-green coffee cups with matching saucers and offered cream, sugar, and a plate of store-bought cookies. They sipped coffee and nibbled cookies while exchanging pleasantries about the weather and answering Mrs. Peterson's questions about their classes. As Beth looked around the room, a splash of orange and blue caught her eye. It was a painting of a man on a horse leading a covered wagon.

"That looks kind of like a painting your sister had," Beth said, pointing.

Mrs. Peterson followed Beth's gaze. "Oh, that? Yes. I know it doesn't match the room, but I can't bear to get rid of it. It's from my dad, you see. He gave each of us kids one of those paintings for Christmas when we were growing up. I guess they reminded him of his youth. He had a fascination with the Old West. He did some roaming around before he got married and settled in Davison City, and he liked to talk about those times. I think he met the artist."

"That was probably why Miss Archer liked to read Westerns so much," Beth said.

"No doubt," Mrs. Peterson said. "She was as fascinated by that time, as was my dad. She often said when she grew up, she wanted to travel and see the places that he described, but she never did."

Evie had been scrutinizing the painting, and she asked, "Is that a Russell?"

"Yes, I think that's the name," Mrs. Peterson said, without much interest.

Turning back to Beth, she asked, "Now, what is this mysterious item that you wanted to show me?"

"As you probably know, Miss Archer left her books to the library," Beth said.

"Yes, her attorney informed us," Mrs. Peterson said.

Beth extracted the card from her book bag and handed it to Mrs. Peterson. "I found this among the books, and I wasn't sure what to do with it. I'd already returned the house key to the attorney, and I didn't want to just throw it away. I thought you might like it."

Mrs. Peterson looked mystified as she took the envelope, opened it, and removed the card. As she gazed at it, her jaw tightened. Mrs. Peterson stared at the card for a long moment, and then she closed it and laid it face down on the table.

"Ah, yes, Jack Cooper. There's a name from the past," she said. Her mouth twisted slightly. "He was a cad." Her voice trembled.

Beth was surprised by her vehemence. "Was he? Why's that?"

"Oh," she waved away the question. "I don't want to speak ill of the dead."

Beth was eager to know more about Jack and why he broke up with Miss Archer, but she couldn't let on that they knew about the break-up without admitting that they'd been snooping, so she didn't pursue the subject.

"Of course. Water under the bridge, I suppose," Beth said. "Tell us more about your and Miss Archer's childhoods. You know, I delivered books to her for years, ever since I was a teenager until just before her passing, but I feel like I never really knew her. We just talked about books. Did your family always live in Davison City?"

"Yes, since the early days of this century. My dad worked in a lumber mill, and he built our house."

Evie asked, "Was the house where Miss Archer lived the family home?"

"That's right." Mrs. Peterson had a faraway look in her eyes. "Of course, we had a much bigger lot when we were kids. My mother used to grow a huge garden that provided the family with vegetables throughout the year." A wistful smile flitted across her face, softening it. At that moment, Beth thought she looked more like her sister. "It was sold off, bit by bit. My parents needed the money. Especially for medical bills after Almira got polio." The stern look returned.

"When was that?" Beth asked.

"The summer of 1916. A polio epidemic hit the Twin Cities when Almira was studying there. If only she'd stayed home . . ." There was a note of bitterness in Mrs. Peterson's voice. Then she hurriedly added, "Not that it was her fault, of course. But she was sick for months, and then she had a limp for the rest of her life. The medical bills had to be paid. So my parents started selling off pieces of our property."

"Was she sick before or after she became involved with Jack?" Beth asked.

Mrs. Peterson was staring into her coffee, as though trying to remember when a door opened somewhere in the back of the house. The sound of the TV grew louder, and a few moments later, Mr. Peterson entered the room.

Mrs. Peterson introduced him to Beth and Evie, while he helped himself to a cup of coffee and a handful of cookies. Holding his snack, he nodded absently and left the room. Once he was gone, Mrs. Peterson's manner changed. Now, she seemed in a hurry to get rid of them.

"Yes, so, the Valentine's Day card. Well, well, very interesting," Mrs. Peterson said. "Thank you for that. Now, if there's nothing else, I need to get supper started."

She continued to talk in a high, artificial tone while Beth and Evie gathered their things and got ready to leave.

Just before they went, Beth turned and asked, "I wonder, did you think that your sister's death was quite sudden?"

Mrs. Peterson paused, and her face hardened, "That's an odd question. No, I didn't. Almira was never strong after she was stricken with polio. I believe her heart was weak for some time. Why do you ask?"

Beth blushed and stammered, "It was just that . . . I thought she seemed fine when I last saw her . . . I wondered, did she call you, or . . . ?"

"No, she didn't call. I'm afraid we weren't that close. I had my own life, my family, and my home. Now, if you'll excuse me." Mrs. Peterson opened the door and stood next to it, like a sentinel, looking determined to end the visit.

Beth and Evie had no choice but to thank her for her time and hospitality and say goodbye.

Once they were back in Beth's car, Evie said, "Boy, she was in a big hurry to get rid of us."

"She sure was. And her manner changed after her husband came into the room. Did you notice? Do you suppose he didn't like Miss Archer?"

"That's possible. Or maybe he didn't like Jack. Or he just didn't like her talking about the old days," Evie said.

Beth pulled her car out of the driveway and started back toward the highway. "Anyway, what were you saying about the painting?"

"I think it's by Charles Marion Russell. I did some research on him, and I found out that he's a pretty well-known Western painter and sculptor."

"Is it valuable?"

"It could be if it's genuine. Of course, it might be a reproduction. I didn't get a close look at it. Even if I had, I probably couldn't tell."

"Okay," Beth paused. "I'm just thinking out loud. Miss Archer had a similar painting by Russell, right? And it may have been replaced by a copy. If that's the case, where is the original? I'm not sure where we go from here."

"Here's an idea—maybe we should talk to Miss Archer's neighbors. I could start tonight," Evie said. "I know you have to work this evening, but I have nothing planned. I could knock on some doors and see if they've noticed people coming and going from her house. It's a quiet street, so any activity probably draws attention. Especially since Miss Archer's death. I bet that caused a stir."

"Good idea," Beth said. "Speaking of causing a stir, an ambulance arriving—assuming that's what happened—would definitely be noticed. If one came, who called it? Did Miss Archer call, or was she with someone else who called? Or did she ask one of the neighbors for help. Ask them about that too. Meanwhile, I'll try to call Sandra and see what she knows about how Miss Archer got to the hospital. Then we can compare notes tomorrow."

Chapter 12

Thursday, March 27

On this day, the twenty-mile trip from Davison City to North Dakota State College was a pleasant drive. It hadn't snowed in days, so the two-lane highway was clear and dry. Spots of black earth poked out of the melting snow in the surrounding fields, promising warmer days ahead. Beth drove with Evie in the passenger seat. The radio was tuned to a top-twenty hits station, and they sang along, off-key, to the Zombies' hit song, "Time of the Season."

After it finished, Evie said, "Wow, what a cool song. It's really different."

"Yeah, I think they call it psychedelic." Beth paused and thought. "I like it. But I kind of miss the old doo-wop songs."

"Me too. But I also like the new stuff. So as I was saying before our duet, I was in Miss Archer's neighborhood yesterday."

"That's right. How did it go? Did you get any good info?"

"Yes, I was lucky. The first person I talked to—her next-door neighbor, Charlene Fleming—was the one who called the ambulance. She said that Miss Archer was alone and started to feel sick, so she called her. Charlene thought it was serious, so she called the ambulance."

Beth turned down the volume of the radio. "Charlene Fleming? The name sounds familiar, but I can't quite place her. Who is she?"

"She's a clerk at the Piggly Wiggly; tall, thin, thirty-something."

"Oh, right. So how was Miss Archer when she got there? Was she able to come to the door?"

"No, but Charlene has a key."

"Another key? I wonder how many are out there."

"I know. Anyway, Charlene found Miss Archer lying on the couch, gasping for air, and starting to turn blue."

"Is that so? In that case, it might have been a heart attack after all. Maybe we're on a wild goose chase."

"Maybe. But Sandra Brown doesn't seem to think so. And then, there's the disappearing will."

"True. And the missing heart pills. I guess I'd like to know about those things before we call it quits."

"I agree. Did you talk to Sandra last night?" Evie asked.

"No. I called her, but no one answered," Beth said. A steady stream of kids came in needing help with their assignments, which are due by the end of the week because next week is their spring break. Kids! Oh well, I remember when I would put things off to the last minute."

Evie laughed. "Yeah, way back when. Like, the last time anything was due. Do you think we'll see Sandra at the fish fry tomorrow?"

"Could be."

"Won't you be working?"

"No, we'll have our normal Saturday hours. Then next week, we're open day hours Monday through Thursday, and closed on the Friday and Saturday before Easter."

"So you'll get some time off?"

"Yeah, tomorrow evening and Easter weekend too. But if I want to pay my rent and eat, I can't afford to take a week off. So I'll work some daytime hours."

"What about your classes?"

"Miss Tanner said I could work around my class schedule. I guess we'll have to drive separately next week."

"No problem." Evie shrugged. "That way I can do some shopping between classes. I need to pick up something for your sister-in-law's baby shower. Any ideas?"

"Oh, right, the baby shower. Thanks for reminding me."

"I can't believe you forgot!" Evie laughed. "Your whole family must be so excited about the baby. Especially your mom, since it's her first grandchild."

"It's practically all she talks about. To the point that it's kind of annoying." Beth pulled a poor-me face. "It's like she's forgotten all about her firstborn." Then she laughed. "But seriously, I'm thrilled to become Auntie Beth. I've just had a lot on my mind."

They drove past the belching smokestacks of the sugar beet plant on the outskirts of East Grand Bend, through town, and across the bridge into Grand Bend, North Dakota.

Evie scanned the river below as they drove over the bridge. "Man, the water is getting high. They're predicting bad flooding this spring."

"That's the last thing we need."

"It was exciting during the last big flood, though, wasn't it? Remember? We were in high school, and when the sirens sounded we were dismissed to help with the sandbagging."

"It sure was. Still, I hope it doesn't get that bad this year. It's not fun for folks whose homes get flooded out."

"And that would certainly happen again. After the last big flood, real-estate developers bought up the lots that were cleared, the houses were torn down, and then new ones were built. I guess they hoped someone would build a dam or something."

"Or they were more interested in making a quick buck than anything else. As far as I know, nothing was ever done for flood mitigation, was it?"

"No. Plans for building dams got bogged down and abandoned. Farmers didn't want to give up valuable crop land."

"So we'll just have to hope for the best," Beth said.

After dropping Evie off, Beth parked behind her apartment and let herself into the kitchen through the back porch. After kicking off her boots and dumping her coat and book bag on a kitchen chair, she put the kettle on for a cup of tea, then poked her head into the living room.

"Hi, Chestnut," she said to the brown-and-tan tabby cat curled up on an afghan, bunched up in the corner of the couch.

He yawned, stretched, and then softly hopped down and padded over.

"Did you miss me?" She leaned down and stroked his back as he rubbed against her legs. "Or do you just want a treat?"

She went over to the kitchen cupboard and got out a small bag of treats and dropped a few into his food dish. He crunched through them and then sat and watched Beth as she made a peanut butter sandwich and a cup of tea.

"I have a half-hour before I have to change for work. Shall we watch a little TV?"

Chestnut tilted his head as if listening. Beth carried her sandwich on a plate and the mug of tea and put it on the end table, shoving aside a pile of newspapers and magazines to make a spot. Then she turned on the TV and settled in to watch an episode of "Father Knows Best." Chestnut jumped up and kneaded a spot on her lap before making himself comfy, and purred until he fell asleep.

The next thing Beth knew, she jerked awake and glanced at her watch. It was only a few minutes before four o'clock. Her mug of tea was cold, and the sandwich was uneaten.

"Oh no!" She jumped up. Chestnut jumped clear, landing on the rug in front of the couch. There he crouched, glowering at Beth.

"Sorry, Chestnut. But I'm going to be late. Miss Tanner will kill me."

She ran into the bedroom and jumped out of her bell-bottom jeans and sweatshirt, threw on a pants-set, and a wide lapel floral shirt under the vest.

This shirt could use a touch-up with an iron, but there's no time for that, she thought.

She ran a comb through her hair, corralling the flyaway strands with a wide headband, and jammed her feet into a pair of pumps. She'd skip changing in and out of boots tonight, and just try to go around the puddles. As she grabbed her purse and coat and ran out the back door, she glanced at her watch, again, and congratulated herself on making the transition in five minutes, a new record.

I'll only be a few minutes late for work, not too bad, she thought. *Maybe Miss Tanner won't even notice.* But she knew that she would.

Beth got into the car, turned the key, and then . . . nothing happened! She swore under her breath and tried again, but still nothing.

"Damn," she shouted. "Stupid car."

How had this happened? She noticed the knob to turn on the lights was pulled out and remembered that the melting snow had created a misty fog on the drive home, so she'd turned on the lights.

Stupid, stupid me. My brother warned me I needed a new battery.

Now what? She could call the library and tell Miss Tanner she would be late, and then call her parents for a ride. Or she could just get there on foot as fast as possible. If she hurried, it would take less than ten minutes. She got out of the car, slammed the door shut, and after aiming a few more curses in its direction, she took off. She ran, then walked until she caught her breath, and then ran again.

When Beth got to the library, she jogged up the stairs to the front door and burst through it, panting and disheveled.

Miss Tanner looked up in astonishment. The forced smile on her face fell. "What on earth is going on, Miss Williams? Don't tell me that you stumbled on another body?"

Beth thought for a moment, and then realized Miss Tanner was referring to when she'd found a murder victim in the park while on her way to work, a few months ago.

"Oh no, nothing like that. I was just running late because my car wouldn't start," Beth said.

"Of course," Miss Tanner said, as she forced a smile. "Beth, may I present the Chairman of the Library Board, Mr. Holte. Mr. Holte, this is my library assistant, Miss Beth Williams, who is normally very prompt and dependable, despite carrying a full class schedule. She is studying Library Science at North Dakota State College in Grand Bend."

"How do you do?" Mr. Holte nodded to her.

Beth turned toward the impeccably dressed man standing next to the circulation desk. "Nice to meet you," she said, and blushed as she suddenly became aware of her dripping shoes and slush-spattered pant legs.

After a few more pleasantries, Beth was dismissed. She went to the librarian's office, where she hung up her coat and purse and checked her appearance in the wall mirror, patting at the unruly shoulder-length brown hair and tucking in a few strands that had come free from her headband. She then applied a quick coat of lipstick before she hurried back out to the circulation desk. Mr. Holte was gone.

Miss Tanner watched her approach with narrowed eyes. "You could hardly have chosen a worse time to show up late and in a disheveled state," she said.

Beth opened her mouth to try to explain, and then shut it again, realizing it wouldn't help. Instead she simply said, "I'm sorry, Miss Tanner."

After all, if she hadn't fallen asleep on the couch, she could have gotten to work on time, even with car trouble. And if she'd turned off the headlights, she wouldn't have run down the battery.

Miss Tanner's manner softened. "That's okay. I'm sorry I snapped. It's just that Mr. Holte came unannounced. He especially wanted to meet you. And I'm a little worried about why. I think the city council is thinking of cutting our funding, and Mr. Holte is investigating ways to handle a cut in our budget. So it was unfortunate timing."

Chapter 13

Friday, March 28

Beth leaned toward Evie. "Father McClure is in his element," she said.

They stood in line at the Friday fish fry, watching the chubby priest, who wore a barbeque apron over his black shirt and pants and white clerical collar, darting around, talking, and laughing to the members of the Men's Club who manned the serving tables. He dashed into the kitchen and then reappeared, wearing oven mitts and carrying a stainless-steel steam-table pan heaped high with deep-fried fillets of fish. He deposited the pan with a satisfying thud in front of one of the servers.

Standing in a line that wrapped around the inside perimeter of the cafeteria of the Catholic high school, Beth felt like she had stepped back in time. The smell of chalk and waxed, wooden classroom floors upstairs provided the base note nearly obscured by the powerful scent of deep-fat-fried fish and French fries that was making her mouth water.

"I hope there's something left by the time we make it through the line," she said.

"Not to worry. I think they only sell tickets for as much food as they have. They've been doing this for years and have it down to a science," Evie said.

Beth scanned the crowd and spotted her mother and sister seated at one of the long tables flanked by folding chairs. She waved to them, and her mother waved back. Cathy, who was deep in conversation with a couple of other teenagers, ignored her.

"Is your dad here?" Evie asked.

"He's probably in the kitchen, elbow deep in the batter. He never misses one of these," Beth said. She scrutinized the crowd again. "Did you see anyone here we should talk to about Miss Archer?"

"Well, there's her nephew." Evie nodded in Melvin's direction. He was sitting at the end of a table with an empty chair in front of him and another between him and a family seated at the other end of the table. "Do you think he'll still be there by the time we make it through the line?"

Beth watched Melvin shoveling in pieces of fish and French fries. "Doubtful. Hold our place and I'll go talk to him now, okay?"

Evie nodded, and Beth made a beeline toward Melvin. "Is this seat taken?" she asked, sitting down without waiting for an answer.

He looked up, startled, then nodded and eyed her, warily, while he finished chewing. "Oh, hello there. Are you here for the fish fry?" he said.

"Yup, I came with Evie." She pointed at Evie, who waved happily at them.

Melvin lifted a limp hand a few inches in her direction and then shoveled in another mouthful.

"I thought I'd come over and say hi. And to tell you again how sorry I was about your aunt's sudden death."

Melvin shrugged and continued to eat.

"I just wish that I had a chance to say goodbye like you did," she said.

His fork paused midway to his mouth and he stared at her with surprise. "What do you mean, like I did?"

"Didn't you get a chance to visit your aunt at the hospital? I thought someone said they saw you there. Did they get that wrong?"

His gaze turned to one of open hostility. "Who said that?" he demanded.

"I can't quite recall. Am I mistaken?"

"Yes, you're *mistaken*. I don't know what you think you're up to, but everyone knows you're a bit odd, going around pretending you're some kind of lady detective. I'd advise you to mind your own business."

Beth felt her face grow hot. "Thanks for the advice." She stood up and pasted a fake smile on her face. "I was just trying to be nice. Sorry to bother you."

He waved her away with his fork, and then attacked another bite of food.

"What was that all about?" Evie asked when Beth rejoined her in line.

Beth turned her back toward Melvin and recounted their conversation and then added, "He was a total jerk about it. I think he has something to hide."

"Yeah, either that or the lady in the hospital room next to Miss Archer's room didn't actually see Melvin at the hospital after all. Maybe she imagined it. Or was dreaming," Evie said.

"Dreaming! More like a nightmare. If he has nothing to hide, why was he so rude?"

"Just being his usual charming self? Anyway, everyone knows he's a bit odd." Evie said, mimicking Melvin's nasal whine.

This made Beth start to giggle. "Stop it! You're awful."

"Did you tell him it takes one to know one?" Evie started to giggle too.

Beth bit her lip and tried not to laugh. The harder she tried, the worse it got, until her shoulders shook with suppressed laughter. It didn't help that, when she glanced at Melvin, he was glaring in their direction. Then she looked at Evie, who mouthed the word "odd." They both shook with suppressed laughter, while Melvin bolted the rest of his food and then raced for the door.

When she could speak normally again, Beth said, "I guess that was kind of childish and mean. Being in this room makes me feel young and silly again."

"Nah, he deserved it."

By this time, they'd made it through the line.

"I'll just say hi to my dad," Beth said.

She stuck her head through the swinging door into the kitchen. It was filled with men in aprons. Beth's dad, with his sleeves rolled up, was mixing up the beer batter. Others were chopping cabbage for coleslaw, dipping fish fillets into the batter and laying them out on trays, and minding the deep-fat fryers. Their faces were flushed from the heat, from sampling the beer, or both.

Beth called out, "Hi, Dad."

He looked up, his apron smeared with batter, and a big smile lit up his heat-reddened face. "Hi, sweetie. I see you made it."

"Yup, I'm here with Evie. Mom and Cathy are here too."

"Yeah, I know. I talked to them earlier. Well, enjoy it."

"You bet. Talk to you later."

Beth rejoined Evie, who handed her a stoneware plate. They moved through the line getting ample helpings of everything and headed back to find Beth's mother and sister.

"Hi, Beth, Evie," her mom said. "We saved you a couple of spots."

They sat down, Beth across from her mom and Evie across from Cathy.

"Hey, Cathy, how's it going?" Beth said.

Cathy looked up and said, "Good." And then she turned back to her friends.

"It looked like you girls were having fun. What was so funny?" Beth's mom asked.

"Oh, nothing. We were just being silly," Beth said.

"Is that so? Was it about Melvin Archer? I saw you talking to him, and then he lit out of here like his pants were on fire."

Mom doesn't miss much, Beth thought. "Yeah, sort of. I said something to him about how it was nice that he got a chance to talk to his aunt one more time before she passed away. For some reason, he took that the wrong way, and his odd reaction struck us as funny. But enough about him. Are Gary and Debbie coming?"

"No. Your brother is working, and Debbie was tired. I think she probably couldn't handle the fried food. Poor thing! She's having kind of a rough time."

"That's too bad," Evie said. "Is it morning sickness?"

"More like morning, noon, and night sickness," Beth's mom said.

"I hope she's feeling better before the baby shower," Evie said. "I found the cutest little layette set for her. It's mint green, so it will work for a boy or a girl."

"That sounds lovely. I'm crocheting a baby blanket. I'm only about half done. It's going slow. I have to concentrate to count the stitches. It's been some time since I last crocheted anything. It's so much fun to have a new baby in the family!" Beth's mom said.

Beth let them gush on about babies. When the subject seemed exhausted, she asked, "It's not like Gary to miss a Friday fish fry. Couldn't he leave Sam in charge of the garage for a couple of hours? Or has Sam gone on another bender?"

"No, I don't think so. That new girlfriend of his keeps him out of trouble," her mom said.

"So it's working out with Sam and Beverly?" Evie asked.

"I think so. She cracks the whip, and he seems to like it," Beth's mom laughed.

"Why didn't Gary leave Sam in charge?" Beth persisted.

"I guess he didn't want to pay him any extra. He needs the money himself, with the baby and his new hobby." Beth's mom rolled her eyes.

"What new hobby is that?" Beth asked.

"Didn't you hear? He bought some old wreck he wants to restore," Mom said. "It's a ten-year-old Corvette—I think—

and it's in pretty rough shape, according to your dad. But Gary just had to have it. He says it's a classic that will be worth a lot of money someday, and it was too good of a deal to pass up."

"What does Debbie think about *that*?" Beth asked.

"She says she understands. But I don't think she's too happy about it. She made Gary promise to only work on it in his spare time. Not that he has much of that," Beth's mom laughed. "Well, they'll work it out. Far be it from me to interfere."

Beth suppressed a smile.

"Mom, what do you know about the early residents of Davison City? The ones who were here when Miss Archer was young. Have you ever heard any interesting tidbits?"

"Tidbits? Such as . . . ?"

"I don't know. For example, Miss Archer had a boyfriend named Jack Cooper. Have you ever heard anything about him?" Beth said.

Evie had been chatting with the couple next to her, but now she leaned toward Beth and her mom to hear the answer.

"I don't know. I'd have to think about it. Why do you ask?" She scrutinized Beth with narrowed eyes.

"Just curious," Beth said. "I'm beginning to realize that I hardly knew Miss Archer, in spite of all of our visits over the years, and I'm trying to fill in the blanks. From what we've pieced together, her boyfriend went off to the war, World

War I that is, and he broke up with her while he was gone. I wondered why."

"You should know. Sometimes things just don't work out."

Beth chose to ignore the dig about her failed relationship with Ernie. "Well, if you think of anything . . ." she trailed off.

"Yes, if I think of anything, I'll let you know." Her mom regarded Beth fondly, and added, "Tell you what, the Crafty Crew is meeting next week. We're making little whatnots for the Easter sale at the church. I'll slip the subject into the conversation and see where it leads."

"Thanks, Mom," Beth said. "You're the best. Oh, one other thing—ask Dad to come over tomorrow morning and jump my battery. Silly me, I let it run down, and I don't want to bother Gary. It sounds like he has enough on his plate. But tell Dad not to come too early. I want to sleep in."

"No work tomorrow?"

"Nope. The library is on holiday hours. So I get a whole weekend off." Beth gestured grandly. "What luxury!"

Chapter 14

Saturday, March 29

Beth sat at her kitchen table in her fuzzy blue bathrobe and slippers and finished her oatmeal and coffee while Chestnut started his breakfast. She noticed the stack of dishes in the sink, sighed, then got up, piled the dishes on the counter, filled the sink with hot, soapy water, and put the dishes back in the sink to soak.

"That will give me a few more minutes to relax," she told Chestnut.

He paused, glanced up at her, seemed to decide it didn't concern him, and went back to crunching his way through his breakfast.

Beth sat down with a second cup of coffee and loaded it down with lots of milk and sugar. Just then, she heard her dad stomping the snow off of his boots in the back porch. He must have finished jumping her car's battery. He came into the kitchen, trailing cold air and the scent of motor oil.

"That'll fix you up for now," he said, and handed her keys back to her. "But you better get a new battery soon. I'll tell your brother to set one aside for you."

"Thanks, Dad," she said. "I don't know what I'd do without you. Tell Gary I'll pick it up when I get paid. Do you have time for a cup of coffee?"

"You bet." He sat down at the kitchen table while she poured a mugful. He turned the book that was on the table around and read the title out loud. "*Prominent People of Davison City.* What's this, a library book?"

"Yeah," Beth sat down across the table from him. "I checked it out from the college library."

"Since when are you interested in local history?"

"I started to get interested when I was checking citations for Mr. Flack's book. And then, after Miss Archer died, I found out stuff about her that I never knew, and I wanted to know more about who was around when she was young."

"What do you want to know?" he asked.

Beth stared into her coffee cup for a moment. "For example, I'd like to find out what happened when she was a teacher. And about the cheating scandal that led to her early retirement."

"Oh, yeah, that was a big deal at the time." Her dad flipped through the book as he drank his coffee, naming people he knew. "There were a lot of characters back in the day, same as now. Not everyone was as upright as this book makes out."

"And," Beth continued. "I found out there was a romance in her past and it ended badly."

"You mean with Jack Cooper," he said, still studying the book.

"You know about that? I asked Mom about it, but she didn't know anything."

"Well, it was before her time—mine too—but I heard about it. Most recently from his sister, Tillie, when I was out at her place doing some roof repair. The breakup was all Miss Archer's fault, according to her version of events. Almira broke her brother's heart."

"His sister!" Beth exclaimed. "Of course. I should have realized he could have family around here. What's her last name?"

"Tillie Damiere. She lives on a farm outside of Plato. She's a widow. I believe her husband died about twenty years ago, and she's been on her own since. They never had any kids."

"What else did she say?" Beth asked.

"Not much. I think she brought that up as her way of saying that if her brother was around, she wouldn't have to pay someone to come out and work on the house. She either doesn't have a lot of money or hates to part with it. It doesn't look like too much has been done on the place in the last twenty years. Although she should be doing okay. She still owns a lot of land. She lives on the homestead and rents out the fields to other farmers. But I guess some folks never got over pinching pennies after the depression."

"Maybe I should give her a call and see what she can tell me."

"I don't think she has a phone. I believe she called me from a neighbor's house. Another one of her thrifty ways," he said, rubbing his fingers together.

"Then maybe I should drop in and see her. Do you think that would be okay?"

He just smiled and shrugged. "She's friendly enough. A little odd from spending so much time on her own, perhaps, but she might like the company."

Beth got the directions, jotted them down, and after her dad left, she gave Evie a call.

"Sounds interesting," Evie said. "Give me a couple of hours to finish helping my mom with the housework. I'll come over when I'm done,"

"Perfect, I need to get a few things done around here too," Beth said.

That afternoon, Evie drove while Beth consulted the notes she made on how to get to Tillie Damiere's farm. They were driving north out of Davison City, following the railroad tracks that headed up toward Canada.

"Turn left at the stop sign just before we get to Plato," Beth said. "We should be almost there."

Plato was a tiny village with a few grain elevators, a gas station, a bar, a small grocery store, and a few other buildings strung out along the highway. A dozen or so homes were hidden behind the businesses.

Beth scanned the flat fields surrounding the road. They were covered with piles of melting, dirt-streaked snow, interrupted by patches of rich, black earth. In the distance, clumps of trees surrounded farmsteads. "The snow is still deep in the ditches."

"Yeah, we got a lot this winter. I hope we don't get any more. They're talking about flooding. My dad said it could be bad this year."

Beth was struck by how much attention they paid to the weather up here. She had lived in the Cities for over a decade, and while there, she'd only cared about the weather in deciding which jacket to wear while dashing to and from her car.

She realized that the local economy depended on farming. Evie's dad wasn't a farmer—he owned a hardware store—but how the farmers did affected his bottom line. Winter snowfalls meant worries about spring floods and delays in planting. Summer hail storms might wipe out the crops. An early fall freeze could spoil the harvest.

Evie slowed at the four-way stop outside of Plato. "Is this where we turn?"

Beth consulted her notes. "Yup, then go two miles and turn left. And it's the first farm on the left."

Beth gazed out at the barren landscape as they bounced along the gravel road. They passed only one abandoned brick house sitting alone in the middle of a field. The windows had either broken out or been removed. She could see right through it.

"I hope she's okay with us dropping in," Beth said. She was starting to feel a little uneasy about this whole trip.

"Your dad thought it would be okay." Evie glanced at Beth and smiled reassuringly. "At worst, we'll waste some time."

"At worst, she'll set the dogs on us," Beth said, and laughed half-heartedly.

Evie turned into the poorly plowed driveway. Straight ahead, a barn listed to the right. A few decrepit outbuildings and pieces of abandoned farm equipment were scattered across the yard. They slowed as the driveway looped in front of the house and then parked.

"We're here. I guess we'll find out." Evie turned off the car, and they sat there for a few moments, waiting and listening to see if anything would happen. When it didn't, they got out and went to the door.

Beth knocked on the screen door, and a dog barked inside the house. As she waited, she noticed the peeling green paint on the doorframe and the gray wood underneath. Her dad was right; the place looked neglected. A tall woman with a cloud of gray hair surrounding her face flung open the inside door, rushed across the porch, and then flung open the screen door. A shaggy, tan dog followed her, wagging his tail.

"Hello," she bellowed. "Who are you, and what do you want?" Without waiting for an answer, she continued. "Don't worry about Buddy. He's one of the world's friendliest dogs. If someone came to rob me, he'd just wag his tail. Wouldn't you, boy? Don't tell me," she peered at Beth with keen blue eyes, "You must be Fred and Martha's girl. I haven't seen you in years."

"That's right, Mrs. Damiere. I'm Beth Williams, and this is my friend Evie Hanson. My dad said it should be okay for us to drop in."

"Yes, yes, I'm happy to see you. And call me Tillie. Everyone does. Come in, come in."

Tillie ushered them into the porch, where, as instructed, they removed their boots and left them on the mat. Then she led them into the kitchen and indicated the coat-tree, where they hung up their jackets.

"It's nice to meet you, Evie, and to see you again, Beth. Your dad told me you were back home. How's that working out for you?"

"Good, good. I don't live at home. I did, for a few months after moving back, but now I have my own apartment and a job at the library. Evie and I are taking classes in Grand Bend."

"Aren't you two a bit old for college?" Tillie forged on. "Well, it's never too late to learn, I always say. Have a seat at the table, and I'll put the kettle on." She gestured toward a round wooden table surrounded by an assortment of old chairs.

After they sat down, Buddy circled their legs, sniffing, and curled up under the table. Tillie rambled on with a steady stream of exclamations and observations while she pumped water into a battered teakettle, lit a burner on the gas stove with a wooden kitchen match, and put the kettle on. Then she sat down at the table and settled her hands in her lap.

"So what's this all about? What brings you girls out for a visit?" she asked, looking back and forth at them.

"My dad mentioned you were Jack Cooper's sister," Beth said.

"Yes, that's right," Tillie said, looking puzzled.

"Well," Beth paused and looked at Evie, unsure how to proceed. "We found a card from Jack, a Valentine's Day card to Miss Archer, when we were packing up her books."

"Packing up her books?" Tillie echoed, looking more puzzled.

"I should explain. Did you know Miss Archer?"

Tillie nodded, no longer smiling. "Yes."

"And that she passed away?"

Tillie nodded again.

"Anyway," Beth said. "Miss Archer left her books to the library, and the card was mixed in with some of the books."

"Oh, I see. So you brought me the card," Tillie said.

"No, sorry. Until my dad told me so this morning, I didn't know that Jack Cooper had a sister. We gave the card to Miss Archer's sister."

"Oh, I see." Tillie frowned. "I suppose that's all right. As you said, you didn't know."

The teakettle whistled, and Tillie jumped up and turned off the burner. She got out a ceramic teapot and a canister, scooped several large spoonfuls of what looked like dried leaves and berries into the pot, poured hot water over it, and then put the pot on the table.

"We'll have to wait a few minutes for it to steep," Tillie said. "I hope you like herbal tea. It's made from hawthorns. They grow around the house."

Beth and Evie both said that they did. Although Beth didn't think she'd ever tried any herbal tea and certainly had not tried hawthorn tea. Tillie quietly moved around the kitchen, fetching cups, spoons, and honey and placing them on the table, seemingly deep in thought. Evie made a few comments about the weather, but there was no response.

"Well, there you are," Tillie sighed, as she resumed her seat. "Jack and Almira. That was a long time ago. Jack was a handsome young man back then. I'll get a picture." Tillie jumped up and charged out of the room and soon returned carrying a framed photo, which she handed to Beth.

Beth examined the sepia-toned photo of a family in their Sunday best, outside of a farm house. The parents were seated—

Beth thought she recognized the chairs as some of those around the table—and a young man and woman stood on either side of them. The parents frowned into the camera. The tall, handsome young man, with ankles and wrists protruding from a suit he'd outgrown, smiled at the camera. The smiling young woman wore an ankle-length light-colored dress with a ribbon around her waist. Her dark hair was escaping from a bun in the back and fanning out around her face. They were all squinting into the sun. Beth handed the photo to Evie.

"So that's you, Jack, and your parents?" Evie said.

"Yes. That was back in 1916. The last summer the whole family was together before Jack went off to war," Tillie said. "Wasn't he handsome?"

"Yes, and you were a lovely young girl," Beth said.

Tillie snorted, derisively. "I was a gawky girl."

"Was Jack younger or older than you?" Evie asked, still examining the photo.

"Two years older." She paused, a faraway look on her face. "He was my big brother. Jack always looked out for me, until Almira came into the picture."

Beth noticed Tillie's mouth twist slightly when she said "Almira."

"Changed how?" Beth asked.

"Oh," Tillie waved a hand dismissively, "he just didn't have time for anyone else."

"I suppose that's normal, a young man in love—" Evie said.

Tillie interrupted, "It was beyond normal. He was gaga over her. I didn't understand it. I still don't. I knew her, you see. She was just an ordinary girl. Nothing special." Tillie's eyes misted up. "You'll have to forgive a silly old lady. What does it matter now?"

Evie looked at Beth and raised an eyebrow as if to say, "Now what?" Beth shrugged almost imperceptibly.

"Yes, well, these things happen," Beth said. "Or so I'm told. Anyway, I've read about it in books. I haven't experienced that kind of thing myself . . ." she trailed off.

"Well, life goes on," Tillie said, loudly as she jumped up. "You girls must be hungry. How about some bread and jam?"

They agreed readily, glad to change the mood. Tillie retrieved a loaf of homemade bread, butter, and a jar of deep red jam. She busied herself at the kitchen counter slicing the bread and then handing around plates of bread, cups of tea, and the other things.

Beth took a tentative sip from her cup. The tea was apple-like, but tart and a little bitter. She doctored it with honey until it was palatable, then spread butter and jelly on her bread and took a small bite.

"This jelly is delicious. What is it?" Beth said.

"That's hawthorn too, but I make it with just the berries. I make up batches of jelly every fall and dry some of the leaves and berries for tea. Might as well make use of what the good Lord provides," Tillie said.

"Yes, indeed," Beth said. "Eating wild foods is becoming more popular these days."

"Right! Like Euell Gibbons," Evie said.

"Who?" Tillie asked.

"He has written books on collecting and eating wild foods. We have some in the library. You should stop in, the next time you come to town, and we can help you check them out," Beth said.

"Well, I don't know. I don't get into town too often. And I don't even have a library card," she said.

"I can take care of getting you a card if you want. And I could bring the books out to you. It's not very far out of my way," Beth said.

Tillie insisted that she didn't want her to go to any trouble, and Beth kept insisting that it wouldn't be any trouble. Finally, Tillie agreed that it might be okay.

Later, when they were back in the car and headed home, Evie laughed and said, "You just can't help yourself, can you?"

"What are you talking about?" Beth said.

"You just have to help an old lady in need of books."

"Oh, I see." Beth laughed. "I suppose so. But I can also pump her for more info on Jack and Almira. I think there's a lot more to the story. Don't you?"

"I get it. Very clever, Holmes. But interesting as it may be, what makes you think it has anything to do with Miss Almira's untimely demise?"

"I'm not sure it does. But let's see where we stand." Beth counted off on her fingers. "We have a missing will, which implies that someone was going to be cut out of the will. That's a possible motive. And we might have a sighting of the nephew at the hospital at the time the will went missing. That all seems very suspicious. But suppose he didn't do it? What other motive could lead someone to kill a seemingly harmless old lady? It must be something in her past."

"That could be." Evie drummed her fingers on the steering wheel. "Like the girl who was expelled, Anna Selvig, seeking revenge. Although she seems to be long gone. Or her parents might blame Miss Archer for ruining their daughter's life. But why would they suddenly seek revenge after all these years?"

"Going back even further, maybe it had something to do with Jack. Like a jealous lover whom he dumped for Miss Archer."

"Or a sister who lost her older brother's doting attention? But that's crazy, right? I mean, for a sister to be so bent out of shape about that after all these years that she suddenly kills his old girlfriend. I don't buy it."

"Yeah, it does seem far-fetched," Beth said. "But then, Tillie is out there, all alone. Maybe she stews over old injustices. Anyway, I got the feeling she's hiding something. If we get to talking, maybe she'll let something slip that will shed new light on things. I have an idea. What if I bring out that *Prominent People of Davison City* book on my next visit, along with a Euell Gibbons book for her, and see if that gets her reminiscing?"

Chapter 15

Sunday, March 30

Beth half awoke and then drifted back to sleep, luxuriating in starting the day slowly. On Sundays, she didn't need to rush off to work or school. She nestled under her comforter and listened to Chestnut purring beside her. She tried to postpone the inevitable, when the call of nature would force her from her cozy cocoon. Gradually, she became aware that it was even quieter than a normal Sunday morning. Then a snowplow roared past her house, startling her to full wakefulness.

She scrambled out of bed and ran across the cold floor. A peek through her bedroom curtains confirmed what she'd suspected—winter had staged a comeback. A thick coating of fresh snow blanketed the ground and roofs of houses. Beth sighed, thinking about shoveling out her car and clearing off the snow before she could drive anywhere.

"You're lucky, Chestnut. You get to stay in and be warm and comfy."

Upon hearing his name, Chestnut opened his eyes halfway, yawned, stretched, and then hopped off the bed, ready to follow Beth around until he got his breakfast.

Beth scuffed her feet into her slippers, wrapped herself in her fluffy, blue robe, and headed to the kitchen to start coffee percolating and to feed Chestnut. Then she took her time getting ready for the day. She was dressed and back in the kitchen when the phone on the wall rang.

It was her dad. "Hi, sweetie. I suppose you noticed that it snowed last night."

"Uh-huh," Beth responded, sleepily.

"Shall we swing by and pick you up for church?"

Beth was a little annoyed by his hovering, but she also didn't want to shovel snow. She stared out of her kitchen window at the shimmering pile of snow where her car should be and watched as a clump of snow slid off of the roof of the house, landing below the window.

"Is it pretty warm out?" she asked.

She knew her dad liked to get up early and that he had probably already been out and about, shoveling snow and making his Sunday morning run to the drugstore for the newspaper.

"Not bad. It's supposed to warm up this afternoon."

"In that case, I think I'll walk."

"Are you sure? We got a lot of snow last night."

"I know. But the snowplow has already come past here, so I can walk in the street if the sidewalks aren't shoveled, and I could use the fresh air. Thanks anyway."

Beth exhaled in relief as she hung up the phone and then poured a cup of coffee. "Sometimes parents are just too helpful," she told Chestnut, who paused and looked at her, meowing as though in agreement.

Beth's walk to church took her past Miss Archer's house. She paused as a shadowy figure inside the house passed by the window. There weren't any footsteps in the snow leading to the front door.

Someone must have come in the back way, she thought.

Beth ran down the snowy driveway to the back of the house. There wasn't a car parked in the back, so they must have come on foot.

Yes, footprints led to the back door.

She cut across the yard and placed one foot into a footstep. *It's someone with bigger feet than me.* She stretched out to match their stride length. *And taller.*

Beth followed the footsteps onto the open back porch and peered through the window of the back door. She didn't see anyone in the kitchen. That wasn't too surprising, since she had glimpsed them in the living room, at the front of the house. She hesitated. Should she knock, just wait and see, or maybe alert the next-door neighbor? And what if someone was there for a perfectly innocent reason? Maybe they came by to check on the house or water the plants, like Miss Archer's sister or nephew, or even the next-door neighbor, Charlene Fleming.

Hadn't Charlene told Evie that she had a key to the place? Beth scanned the snow between Charlene's house and here. No, the snow was undisturbed between the houses. It wasn't her.

Beth peeked through the window of the door again, but she still didn't see anyone. Then she placed an ear against the glass. Someone was moving around inside.

Suddenly, the door flung open, knocking Beth backward. She slipped on the slushy snow and landed flat on her back, with the breath knocked out of her. Her head banged down on the porch floor. Stunned and disoriented, Beth struggled to get up. As she got to her feet, her assailant disappeared behind the garage and ran down the alley. Beth jumped up and ran after them. She crossed the backyard to the alley and looked in the direction they had gone. No one was there. They must have gone between one of the houses.

Beth turned and ran back toward the front of the house, hoping to catch a glimpse of them. Then she heard a car start up and accelerate away from her. She'd missed them!

She brushed snow off her coat as she walked to the back door of the house. It had been left hanging open when the intruder fled. Beth let herself in and closed and locked it behind her.

Beth slipped out of her boots and left them on the rug by the back door.

The previous visitor hadn't bothered to take a similar precaution. Beth followed the wet footprints through the kitchen, dining room, and into the living room, where they disappeared into the carpet. She stooped down, as she crept along, and felt for dampness. The damp spots led her through the living room and into the study. There, they seemed to stop just short of the bookcase. Beth felt around in all directions, but this seemed to be as far as they went. She stood upright and was facing a bright oil painting on the wall.

Beth examined it. It looked the same as before, but different. A cowboy on horseback sat on a rock outcropping and stared off into the sun setting over the white, snowcapped mountains. But the colors seemed brighter. Beth decided to take a quick look around the house.

Nothing else seemed out of place. She checked the medicine cabinet to see if the bottle of pills might have reappeared, but there was still an empty spot where the bottle had been.

"Yoo-hoo! Is someone here?" A woman's voice called out.

Beth quickly shut the medicine cabinet and ran down the stairs. The next-door neighbor leaned into the house, regarding Beth with suspicion. "Who are you?" she asked.

"I'm Beth. Beth Williams."

"Oh, right. You're Evie's friend, aren't you? I've seen you around."

"That's me. And you're Charlene Fleming, right?"

"Uh-huh. How did you get into the house?"

"The door was open. I was walking by and I saw someone in the house, so I came in to investigate—"

"You mean they left the door open?"

"Well, sort of. Like I was saying, someone was in here, and I was trying to look into the kitchen to see who it was. Then they ran out so fast they knocked me over." Beth pointed to the disturbed patch of snow on the porch.

"Did you see who it was?"

"No. I was kind of stunned, I guess. I only caught a glimpse. You didn't see anyone, did you?"

"No, sorry. I try to keep an eye on the place—water the plants, and so on—but I can't always watch."

"I'm sure not. Well, I should be going. I was on my way to church, and now I'm going to be late." Beth pulled her boots back on.

"Speaking of watering the plants . . ." Charlene stepped into the kitchen. "I should check them. They look droopy. I don't know why I bother. I checked with the sister and the nephew, and neither of them wants the plants. I don't either. I don't suppose you'd take them."

Beth glanced at the violets. They looked pathetic and in need of help. In fact, most of them looked beyond hope. Miss Archer would have been appalled. But maybe a couple of them could be saved. Not that she'd had any experience with violets. However, there were probably books she could consult. And that lady she met at the fish fry who had been a friend of Miss Archer's. What was her name? It was a bird. Oh yes, Mrs. Wren.

"I can try, I suppose. But I can't take them right now. I can stop by your house this afternoon and pick them up, if that's okay."

"Great! But not today. I have to go to work. Give me a call," Charlene said. "My number's in the book. I'll just check around before I lock up."

"Okay, see you later," Beth said.

She finished walking to church and tiptoed in just before the Gospel reading. She took a seat in the back, hoping no one noticed her late entrance.

Chapter 16

Sunday Evening, March 30

Beth was on the phone with Evie when someone knocked on her door.

"Someone's at the door. I'll talk to you tomorrow," she said.

She opened the door and was surprised to find Bill Crample standing there. He was out of his cop uniform, and his pick-up truck was parked on the curb rather than his squad car.

"Hi, what brings you by?" she asked.

"Just wanted to have a chat, if that's okay," he said, avoiding eye contact. "I tried to call, but no one answered, and then the phone was busy. I was in the neighborhood, so . . ." he trailed off.

"Oh, sure. Come on in." Beth stepped aside and gestured him in. "Can I get you a cup of coffee or something?"

She tried to think of what else she could offer him. She had a half-empty bottle of wine that had been sitting in the cupboard for some time. She didn't have any beer, which, based on what he'd ordered on their only date, was more to his taste.

"Nothing, thanks." He stood on the floor mat, looking uncomfortable.

"Well, come on in and take a seat anyway."

He wiped his feet and went and sat down on the couch. Chestnut cautiously approached him, sniffed at his pant legs, and then hopped up into his lap.

"He must remember you," Beth said.

"Yeah," was all he said, as he scratched behind Chestnut's ears.

Beth was annoyed by his reticence. It was such a chore to have a conversation with him, so she decided to just sit in silence and wait for him to announce what he wanted.

Bill didn't say anything for a few more moments, harrumphed a couple of times, and then said, "I happened to talk to Charlene Fleming at the grocery store today."

"Oh?"

"Yeah, she mentioned that she found you inside Miss Archer's house."

Beth felt her face grow hot. "Is that right? Did she tell you how I happened to be in the house?"

"She said you claimed you saw someone in the house, and when they left they left the back door open."

"Claimed? She said I claimed?" Beth heard her voice go up and felt her hands start to shake.

"Well, maybe she didn't use that word."

"Did she add that the person knocked me over when they fled the house and ran down the alley?"

"No, she didn't. Were you hurt? Are you okay?"

"Yeah, I'm okay." Beth was touched by his concern.

"Did you see who it was?"

"No. By the time I got up and chased after them, they'd disappeared. They must have run between the houses. So then I went back and checked around the house to see if anything was amiss."

"Was it? Was anything missing?"

"Not missing—added."

Bill looked confused.

Beth laughed. "This is going to sound weird, but there was a different painting on the wall in the study than the one that was there when Evie and I were boxing up the books."

"Are you sure?" he asked.

"Pretty darn sure. It was a brightly colored painting with a Western theme. It is the same picture, but it looks too new."

"How about before, when you were visiting Miss Archer? Was it there then?"

"I'm not sure. As far as I can recall, I never went into that room when I visited her. We either sat in the dining room or the living room."

"That *is* weird," Bill said. "What do you suspect?"

"I'm not sure. I think it has something to do with Miss Archer's death."

Bill looked at her, eyebrows raised, and the story came tumbling out.

She told him how Miss Archer had gotten sick and called her neighbor, Charlene Fleming, who had called the ambulance. How Sandra Brown had asked her to investigate because of the missing will. And now a painting vanished, suddenly reappeared, and then changed into a different painting. Bill just listened and nodded as she spoke. Beth concluded, "So you see, there are a lot of mysterious events surrounding Miss Archer's death."

Bill thought for a couple of minutes as he continued to stroke Chestnut, who was purring in appreciation. "Do you want to go over there now and show me the painting?" he asked.

"Really? Now?" Beth said.

"Sure. Why not? I'll need to swing by the station and pick up the key, but that won't take long."

"Okay if I call Evie and have her meet us there?"

He shrugged. "I guess so. But why?"

"She's an art major, and I'd like to have her take a look at it, too. It seems to me there's something off about it. That it's too bright for an old painting."

Bill shrugged in agreement, so Beth called Evie and asked her to meet them at Miss Archer's house, and to bring a camera loaded with colored film. That way, Beth figured, if the painting went missing again, at least they'd have a record of it.

Shortly thereafter, they were in Miss Archer's house examining the painting.

"See what I mean?" Beth pointed at the painting. "It doesn't look like it's over sixty years old, does it?

Evie found the light switch and turned on the overhead light, and then looked more closely at the painting. "I think you're right. To my eye, it looks like a reproduction, and a very recent one at that." She started to snap pictures.

Bill stared at it with narrowed eyes. "Why would anyone sneak into a house to hang a painting? Didn't you say you never had a close look at it until recently?" he asked Beth.

"Yes, that's true," Beth said.

"So what if it is a reproduction? Maybe that's all it ever was, and you just didn't notice it until now."

Beth thought back, trying to be sure. "Well . . . I guess I don't know."

Evie said, "I'm sure this is different than the one that was here when we packed up the books. I'm studying art, and I would swear that this is not the same painting."

"Okay, so what if it was gone and now it's back? Maybe it has nothing to do with the person who was in the house earlier today," Bill said.

"I suppose that's possible," Beth said. "But they were up to something, and it wasn't anything good, based on how they ran out of here. And nothing else looks out of place. Not that I got a chance to check, thoroughly, or that I know exactly where everything should be. But I looked around some."

"Her medication was still gone. Right?" Evie asked.

Bill looked from one to the other. "What's this about medication?"

"There was some prescription medication in the bathroom cabinet when we were first here, and then it was gone when we came back. Someone removed it," Beth said.

"You've been doing a lot of snooping around, haven't you? Didn't I tell you to stay out of it?" He glared at Beth.

Beth glared back. "I was asked to look into it. And I wouldn't have to snoop around, as you put it, if the police were interested in doing their job."

"Don't tell me how to do my job," Bill said.

"I was the one who checked the medicine cabinet the first time," Evie interrupted. "If that was a mistake, blame me."

Bill ignored Evie and continued to glare at Beth. "If there was any evidence, you've destroyed it by trampling all over it and getting your fingerprints on everything."

Beth took a couple of deep breaths and thought for a moment. "Not on this." She pointed to the picture. "I haven't touched it. If this is a clue, you can take it in for fingerprinting."

He shook his head and let out an audible sigh. "Okay. If it makes you feel any better. I'll get someone to come out and dust it for prints—call it suspected art forgery. I'll probably get a reputation as a kook. Serves me right . . ." he trailed off. "Anything to shut you up. Happy?"

"I will be if you can get them to dust the medicine cabinet for prints too," Beth said.

"That's a waste of time. It's bound to be smeared with all sorts of prints, including yours."

Beth opened her mouth to argue. Before she could speak, he held up a hand, and said, "Okay, we'll check it out, just to say we did. I might need fingerprints from both of you to eliminate them. If so, I'll let you know," Bill said.

He wandered over to the phone, mumbling, "I wonder if this is still in service." He picked up the receiver and then nodded when he heard the dial tone.

Turning to them, he said, "Now, if you don't mind, get out of here and let me do my job."

"Gladly," Beth said.

She and Evie went out the back door.

"Have you gone to the Art Restoration and Conservation store in Grand Bend yet?" Beth asked.

"Not yet. Every time I try to stop in, either they're not open or something comes up. But I'll keep trying," Evie said.

Chapter 17

Monday, March 31

Beth wandered into the stacks searching for the two Euell Gibbons books held by the Davison City Public Library. She wasn't used to working in the morning. She yawned, in spite of the two cups of coffee she'd had before leaving home.

Beth heard Miss Tanner talking in her office. No one was with her, so she must be on the phone. Wide awake now, Beth strained to hear. She couldn't make it out, but Miss Tanner sounded upset. Her voice went up in pitch and grew louder. Then Beth heard the telephone receiver slam down.

Beth found the Gibbons books, took them back to the circulation desk, checked them out to herself, and stashed them in her book bag under the counter. She'd bring them out to Tillie's house on her next visit. Beth planned to swing out to her house on her way home from school sometime in the next few days, since she wouldn't have to rush to work after classes. She'd bring a library card application form with her. That way, if Tillie wanted to borrow the books, she could apply for a library card, and then Beth could check the books back in and check them out to Tillie the next time she was at work.

Oh, the power of a library assistant. Beth chuckled at the thought.

But before taking any side trips, she'd have to stop at her brother's shop and pick up the new car battery he had waiting for her. Which would mean eating lunch while driving to college, but that was preferable to risking a dead battery. Not that she could pay for the battery until after payday. She was sure he would accept a post-dated check—one advantage of doing business with your little brother.

Beth was going through the due-date cards and preparing overdue letters when she heard Miss Tanner's office door open and her high-heeled shoes tapping loudly and rapidly in her direction. Beth turned and caught sight of her as she emerged from the non-fiction stacks. Her red bouffant hairdo was quivering and her cheeks were flushed.

She marched around to the side of the circulation desk and paced back and forth, muttering to herself, and then stopped abruptly.

"I am not going to put up with this," she announced and resumed pacing.

"Put up with what?" Beth asked.

"I just got off the phone with Mr. Holte, the Library Board Chairman. Remember him?"

Beth nodded. "Of course. What did he want? Was it about funding?"

"Yes, it was about funding." Miss Tanner's shoulders dropped. She pushed through the swinging door into the circulation area and sank into the chair next to Beth's. "As I feared, the city council wants to cut our funding. He said they don't care if that means cutting hours! Can you believe that?" Her jaw was clenched, and fire shot from her eyes.

"Is it final?" Beth asked, as she imagined herself serving burgers at the Big Boy.

"Not if I have anything to say about it." Miss Tanner squared her shoulders and straightened up. "I intend to rally our supporters to attend the next city council meeting. You will have to be there too, of course. It might mean your job."

"When is the meeting?" Beth asked.

"In a few weeks, on a Saturday. That gives me time to make calls and send out flyers to rally the library supporters."

"But I'll be working that Saturday," Beth said, hoping to avoid a confrontational meeting.

"We'll just have to open late. We'll post signs about the change in hours, well in advance, with the reason for opening late and information about the meeting. That should get even more people to show up."

Miss Tanner's cheeks were still red, but now her blue eyes twinkled behind her tortoise-shell glasses. It looked like she relished the prospect of a good fight.

The bell jangled as Beth pushed through the door of Dave's Auto Repairs. The shop was named after the original owner. No one was at the battered metal desk in the waiting room.

A few moments later, after the clanking of dropped tools, Sam, the part-time employee, emerged from the garage wiping his oily hands on a blackened rag.

"Beth!" he said with a rakish smile. "What brings you in?"

"Hi, Sam. I need a new battery. Is my brother here?" she said.

"Yup. Hang on, I'll get him," he said.

He leaned back through the door and called out, "Gary, your sister is here for her battery." Turning back to Beth, he said, "So what's new with you?"

"Not much. School, work, the usual. You? Still going out with Beverly?"

He looked down at his hands and bit his lower lip, "Yeah." A slow smile spread across his face. "Yeah, Bev and me, we're kinda going steady."

Beth guessed his earlier flirtatiousness was just out of habit. He was her same age and had always been kind of a wolf. If he was settling into a long-term relationship with Bev, it would be the first in a long while.

"Good to hear," she said.

Just then, her brother appeared alongside Sam, also wiping grease off his hands. "Come on back and see my new toy," he said, gesturing into the garage.

"Oh, yeah," Sam said. "You're going to love this."

Beth doubted it, and she was eager to get on with things. But she didn't want to be rude, so she trailed behind them into the garage.

"There it is." Gary pointed at an old red-and-white sports car he had on one of the hoists.

"Oh, right! Mom said you bought an old sports car to work on, as sort of a hobby."

He started to walk around it pointing out various features, with Sam trailing behind and making admiring comments. It was a 1959 Corvette. Beth absorbed that much. Most of the other technical details went over her head.

"I'm dropping the motor. It needs new rings and pistons."

"Won't that be terribly expensive?"

"Not at all. The parts are cheap, and I have all the tools I need."

"When will you find the time?"

Gary stopped and frowned at her.

"Well, back to work," Sam said, making a discreet exit.

"Say, what's all this? Did Mom put you up to asking all these questions?"

Beth laughed. "Nope, I thought of them all by myself."

He looked at her skeptically.

"Okay, so Mom said *something*. She's just worried that you'll neglect Debbie or the baby."

Gary's usually friendly face hardened. "I would never do that!"

Beth waved her hand back and forth as if to say, erase that. "No, no, of course not. And Mom didn't actually *say* that. That was just my interpretation. What she did say was that you got a good deal. I suppose it's an investment."

Mollified, Gary resumed telling her about his plans for sourcing parts and showing the car when it was finished. "Maybe I'll give it to my son one day," he finished.

"Or your daughter."

He laughed derisively and said, "I'm hoping for a son at some point. Not a girl's kind of thing, is it? But if she's into it, sure, maybe I'll give it to my daughter."

"I would love to spend more time hearing all about your new car," Beth lied, "but I need to get to my afternoon classes. Can you install my new battery now?"

"Sure," Gary said.

It took him only a few minutes to replace her battery while Beth waited inside the shop. When he came in, she asked him how much and wrote out the check. "But don't cash it until next week. After I get paid."

"Okay, no problem."

Beth carefully tore the check out of her checkbook and handed it to him, wondering how many more paychecks she would get from the library.

"I heard about Miss Archer. I'm sorry about her passing. I know she was a friend of yours."

"Yeah, thanks. It was a shock. She seemed fine the last time I saw her. Sandra Brown—you know, the nurse— asked me to look into it."

"You? Why you?" Gary rang open the cash register and stashed her check under the cash drawer.

"Because of the Crystal Jones case, I suppose. She seems to think there was something fishy about Miss Archer's death."

"Was there?"

"I don't know. Maybe, maybe not. I've talked to Miss Archer's sister and nephew and Tillie Damiere."

"Tillie Damiere?" He looked startled. "Why her?"

"She's the sister of Miss Archer's old flame. I thought she might tell me something about a motive for murder. If that's what it was. Something from the old days, before I met her. The Miss Archer I knew didn't have any enemies."

"How did you know she had a connection with Miss Archer?" he asked.

"Dad told me. He was out at her house recently, doing some work on her roof."

"Huh, that's interesting. Tillie was in here not too long ago. She has an old Ford truck she drives. She comes into town once in a blue moon to get supplies. The tires were nearly bald. She finally had them replaced."

"She was in town? When was that?"

"Let me see." He went over to the battered filing cabinet, opened a squeaky drawer, and pulled a file. He glanced through it. "It was on Thursday, the thirteenth of this month."

Beth thought for a few moments. "She didn't mention that. That was the day before Miss Archer suddenly fell ill and then died."

Chapter 18

Monday, March 31

Beth decided to postpone the side trip to Tillie's until she'd talked it over with Evie. Why had Tillie concealed the fact that she was in Davison City shortly before Miss Archer's death? Did she have something to hide? Surely, it couldn't have just slipped her mind.

She decided that instead she would stop at Charlene Fleming's house, pick up the African violets, and ask her about her conversation with Bill Crample. Beth fumed thinking about it. It was pretty crummy of Charlene to make it sound like she'd broken into Miss Archer's house.

Beth headed home, turning west onto the two-lane highway that passed between fields of barren, black dirt dotted with puddles of melted snow that reflected the overcast sky, which was stretched out like a dome around her. A misty rain began to fall, dimpling the puddles. None of this helped her mood. She flipped on the radio and sang along, trying to cheer up.

Her thoughts drifted to the book she'd checked out from the college library. It was about caring for houseplants, with a chapter on African violets. She'd scanned through it and had not been reassured. Violets required just the right amount of light, a particular kind of potting soil, regular fertilizing, and more. She'd never had much success with houseplants and wondered if she was up to the job of reviving Miss Archer's violets. Even if she did, Chestnut might knock them over or walk on them. But since they currently seemed doomed, she might as well try.

Soon, Beth stood on Charlene's open front porch. She knocked on the door and stomped the slush off of her boots. She heard footsteps approaching and pasted a smile on her face as the door opened.

"Hi, Charlene. I was just passing by and thought I'd pick up the plants now, if this is a good time." Beth heard a television blaring in the background. It sounded like a soap opera.

"Come on in. Hang on, I'll just turn off the TV," Charlene said.

Beth stood on the entry rug, while Charlene trotted over to the TV set sitting on a wire cart, topped by a ceramic bird sculpture and a vase of artificial flowers, and flipped it off.

"I hope this isn't a bad time. It looks like you were in the middle of a program."

"Don't worry about it. It's just *Days of Our Lives*. I could miss a week and still keep up with the story." Charlene laughed. "Not that I ever miss a week. It's sort of an addiction, I guess. Do you have time for a visit, or are you rushing off to work?"

"Nope, I'm on my way home."

"Oh, good. So you can stay. I'll just put some coffee on."

"Don't go to any trouble on my account."

"No trouble, I was just about to make a pot," Charlene insisted.

They argued about it for a few more moments until Beth agreed to stay. She took off her things and trailed Charlene through the dining room, where Beth noticed a cardboard box containing the African violets sitting on the dining room table, and into the kitchen.

Charlene's house had much the same layout as Miss Archer's house did. The windows of her dining room had a clear view of Miss Archer's front porch, and the kitchen window, over the sink, overlooked her back door.

"Have you seen any people coming and going, recently, over at Miss Archer's house? Besides me, I mean," Beth said, keeping her voice friendly.

Charlene blushed. "It sounds like you talked to Bill Crample."

"Yeah. He stopped by to ask me about it. He said he talked to you in the grocery store and you claimed that I broke in. I suppose he was exaggerating." Beth forced a small laugh.

Charlene avoided looking at Beth and busied herself with preparing the coffee and putting some lemon bars on a plate.

"I don't remember my exact words. We were just talking, you know how it is. Maybe I made it sound like more than it was. Sorry about that."

"That's okay. We went over and checked out the house. So besides Bill Crample, Evie, and me, who else have you seen coming and going from Miss Archer's house? Did you see who ran out of there and knocked me over?"

"No, I didn't see them. Let me think. Who else have I seen?" Charlene counted off on her fingers. "Her nephew was over often, of course. And before she got sick, there were deliveries from the drugstore and the grocery store."

"So you didn't deliver her groceries."

"Not usually, no. Just an occasional bottle of milk, or whatnot, when she ran out. She had a regular weekly delivery. The postman came nearly every day, of course. And her sister dropped by once in a while. Her friend from the African Violet Society, Mrs. Wren, used to pick her up and take her to the monthly meetings."

"Oh, yes, Mrs. Wren," Beth said. "I met her at the funeral lunch. Maybe I'll call her for advice on the plants." *And maybe she'll tell me something about Miss Archer's past that will explain her mysterious death,* she thought.

"That's about it, I think. There could be others. It's not like I'm always watching. But as you said, I have a good view of her house."

"Of course."

"Since her passing, I've been trying to keep a closer eye on the place. Watering the plants and so on." She paused while plating the bars. "Come to think of it, there was another visitor just before she got sick. I saw her leave. At first, I thought it was Miss Archer's sister, but she was taller. I didn't get a good look, so I'm not sure who she was."

"So it was a woman. Did you see her car?"

"No, I don't think she drove there. I saw her walk away."

"Maybe another old friend. By the way, have you ever noticed the painting in Miss Archer's study?"

There was a pause. "A painting?" Charlene looked off to the side as though considering the question. "I don't think so. Why?"

"It's just kind of a puzzle. It seems brighter than I remembered." Beth stared out of the window at Miss Archer's house and then shook her head to clear it. "I might be imagining things. I never got a really good look at it until after her death, because I never went into that room."

"Is that so," Charlene said, without much interest. "Come on, let's sit in the dining room while the coffee perks."

She led the way, carrying the plate of bars and a handful of paper napkins, set them at one end of the table, and shoved the box down to the other end.

"I'll be happy to give these plants to you. I just don't have a green thumb. That's why I like artificial flowers." She gestured toward those sitting on top of the TV set.

Chapter 19

Monday, March 31

Beth placed the African violets on her kitchen counter, three on each side of the north-facing window. Not a great location, but it would have to do until she could figure out a better place. Maybe she would reconfigure her bricks-and-boards shelving to create an area for them in the living room, under the east-facing window. Meanwhile, leaving the over-the-sink fluorescent light on during the day should help. Just as she feared, Chestnut immediately jumped up on the counter and started sniffing the plants.

"Down, Chestnut." She picked him up and plopped him onto the floor. "We have to be nice to the plants and see if we can help them grow."

"Meow," he said as he looked at her skeptically.

"I know, I doubt it too. But if you chew on them or tip them over, that certainly won't help. So leave them alone. There's a good kitty."

She dug the bag of kitty treats out of the cupboard and dropped a few in his bowl. While he crunched through them, Beth called Evie and asked her to come over after supper to discuss the latest developments. Then she popped a TV dinner into the oven.

She was about to head into the living room to watch the evening news when her phone rang.

"Hello?"

"Hi, Beth, this is Sandra Brown."

"Oh, Sandra, it's been a while. I've been meaning to call you and catch up. How have you been? What's new at the hospital?"

"Not much. We still haven't found the will. How about you?"

"Not a whole lot here, either, just a few small things I'm curious about. Evie is coming over later to talk through what we know and what we think it means. Want to join us?"

Sandra agreed, and Beth called Evie back and told her Sandra was coming.

"Can you stop by the grocery store and pick up some chips or something? I have half a bottle of wine, and some tea, or coffee," Beth said.

"Red or white wine?" Evie asked.

"It's a cabernet, I think."

"In that case, I'll get grapes, cheese, and crackers, instead of chips. Chips go with white wine or beer."

"Sounds good. Very classy."

While her TV dinner was baking, Beth tidied up. She moved piles of magazines and newspapers from the coffee table to the bookcases, threw one of her grandmother's afghans across the couch to cover most of the cat hair, and then bolted her dinner when it was ready.

After her friends arrived, the three women helped themselves to wine and snacks in the kitchen and then carried plates and glasses into the living room. Evie and Sandra sat on the couch with Chestnut curled up between them. Beth took the chair across from them.

"I noticed that you have Miss Archer's African violets in the kitchen," Evie said. "Does that mean you stopped at Charlene's house?"

"Yup. On my way home today," Beth said. "I decided to postpone going out to Tillie's."

Sandra looked questioningly from Beth to Evie.

Beth explained who Charlene was. "She's been keeping an eye on the house and caring for her African violets. But she hasn't had much luck with them, so she gave them to me. I don't expect to have much luck either. I don't suppose you know anything about growing them."

"Sorry, no. I don't have pets or plants," Sandra said. "I work such weird hours at the hospital that I can't take care of anything or anybody except myself. And who's Tillie?"

Evie told her that Tillie was the sister of Miss Archer's long-ago boyfriend, Jack Cooper.

"She lives on a farm near Plato," Beth said. "My dad remembered her. Evie and I recently visited her. I was going to stop by and bring her some library books today, but I decided to pick up the plants instead."

"Do you think Tillie has anything to do with the case?" Sandra asked. "Surely, a relative anxious to inherit is the most likely suspect. If only we could find the will. It might reveal who was about to be cut out of their inheritance, and they would be the prime suspect."

Beth smiled. "That's true. It sounds like you're another mystery buff, Sandra. But while we wait for the missing will to turn up, if it ever does, we might as well fill in some of the blanks about Miss Archer's past. Maybe we'll discover another motive."

"For example, the cheating scandal," Evie said.

"Oh, you mean back when she was a teacher?" Sandra said.

Beth and Evie nodded.

Evie turned to Beth. "You never knew that, until recently, in spite of knowing her for many years. She never talked about it. Right?"

"She never talked about herself. We've learned a lot of new stuff about Miss Archer since she passed away," Beth said.

"I remember that scandal," Sandra said. "It was a big deal at the time. Anna completely went off the rails, and Mr. and Mrs. Selvig were so embarrassed they became somewhat reclusive for a time."

"Hang on, let me get a notebook and write this stuff down," Beth said. She left the room and, after some shuffling of papers and opening and closing of drawers and doors, reappeared with a notebook and a pencil, settled back into her chair, and drew some columns down the sheet of paper.

"So I'm going to put down a date, if known, the events, and the names of suspects.

Beth wrote, "1947, cheating scandal, Selvigs." "I suppose that both Mr. and Mrs. Selvig are suspects. Anna would be, too, but she's disappeared. What else?"

"There's the missing will, obviously," Sandra said. "Let me think. It was March 14 when Miss Archer died, wasn't it? And the woman in the next room, Mrs. Schaffer, saw someone she thought might be Melvin Archer, in the hallway that night."

"But didn't you say that Mrs. Schaffer has dementia?" Beth said.

"Yes. But she fades in and out. Sometimes she's perfectly lucid," Sandra said.

Beth nodded and made notes. "Maybe we should visit her. We might get lucky and she may remember more." Beth said.

"Yeah." Evie nodded in agreement.

"Is Mrs. Schaffer still in the hospital?" Beth asked Sandra.

"At the moment. We had to wait for a nursing home bed to open up before we could discharge her because her family isn't able to care for her any longer. We finally found a place, and she's going to be moving in the next few days."

"Okay, so maybe we should go tomorrow afternoon," Beth said. "Before the move, which might confuse her even more."

"Sounds good," Evie said.

"As for the will, I guess the relatives would be the likely suspects. That would be the nephew and the sister. Right?" Beth wrote their names in her notebook.

"Right," Evie said. "Although the sister seems pretty well off, judging from her house. Melvin always looks shabby. Maybe he needs money badly enough to kill for it."

Sandra snorted derisively. "Not really. Rumor has it he's loaded. He inherited his parents' house free and clear, and he rarely spends on anything."

"I can believe that," Beth said. "Of course, if he's greedy or miserly, he might still kill for money. What else?" Beth sipped some wine and popped a grape into her mouth.

"Well, there's the painting," Evie said.

"What's this about a painting?" Sandra asked.

Beth explained, concluding, "Each time Evie and I have gone into her house, these past couple of weeks, something different was going on with the painting. First, it was gone. We could see a darker spot on the wall where it had been hanging. I sort of remembered it being there, though I never paid much attention to it. Then, when we went to pack up her books, it was hanging there again. But the next time we saw it, it looked like a slightly different painting."

"By the way, I finally was able to visit the Art Restoration and Conservation store. Interesting place," Evie said.

"Art restoration store?" Sandra echoed.

"Beth and I saw a check Miss Archer had made out to that store," Evie said. "We guessed she'd sent her painting out for conservation. I'm trying to look into it. The first couple of times I stopped by, it wasn't open, even though the posted hours indicated that it should be."

"Did they explain why they were closed?" Beth asked.

"Yeah, the owner said her employee, a Miss Flambois, has been missing a lot of work lately. So she closes up when she needs to run errands," Evie said. "That got me thinking, maybe I should get a part-time job in the store."

"You should," Beth said. "It would be great experience for you. Did you volunteer?"

"I didn't want to get Miss Flambois fired, so I just kind of hinted around that I might be interested. I let her know I was an art student and that it seemed like it would be an interesting place to work."

"Let's get back to the painting. What did you find out about it?" Beth said.

"You would have been proud of me, Beth. I was very covert about it." Evie grinned. "I implied that Miss Archer told me she was having restoration work done on her painting. I said my mother was thinking of having something similar done, and I inquired about the process and the cost to make it seem like a legitimate inquiry. The owner confirmed that they had worked on Miss Archer's painting. And that Miss Flambois had delivered the painting when it was done. Since Miss Archer had mobility issues, they picked it up and delivered it, which is not a normal part of their service."

"Wow!" Beth looked at Sandra and Evie. "I guess that explains why the painting was gone. But not when and how it was returned. Or if it was later replaced. Do you think it might be the same painting, but we were fooled by the restoration work or a change in lighting?"

"Maybe," Evie said, doubtfully, as she swirled the wine in her glass. "I suppose it is possible that when they cleaned it, some of the paint came off, and it was retouched so much that it turned out looking like a reproduction. I'd have to show it to the shop owner to get a definitive answer."

"Or show it to one of your art professors," Beth said. "But Bill Crample probably won't let us have it now that it's evidence.

Meanwhile, what about the photos you took? Have they been developed? You could show those to people, including Miss Archer's sister. She would be familiar with the painting."

"Yeah. A couple of the photos are pretty sharp. I'll pursue the art angle. That's a good idea," Evie said.

Beth consulted her list. "Okay, here's what we have for clues so far: the painting, the will, and the cheating scandal. Anything else?"

"Don't forget the missing medication," Evie said.

Beth briefly explained it to Sandra as she made notes. She concluded, "The medication went missing between our first and second visit to the house."

"I can try to find out what medication she was on and let you know when you visit the hospital tomorrow," Sandra said.

"Great idea," Beth said. She set down her empty glass. "I'm all out of wine, but does anyone want tea or coffee?"

"I'd take a cup of tea," Evie said.

"I can't. I have to be up early tomorrow. I'll see you tomorrow," Sandra said, getting up to leave.

Once she was gone, Beth and Evie moved to the kitchen table. Beth put on the teakettle.

"There were sure a lot of mysterious comings and goings to Miss Archer's house," Beth said. "Which reminds me: I found out that Tillie was in town the day Miss Archer got sick."

"Really? She didn't mention that. How did you find out?"

"Gary told me when I picked up my new car battery. He worked on her car that day." Beth stared off into space for a moment. "That reminds me, Charlene said she saw a woman she didn't recognize leaving Miss Archer's house, on foot, that same day. Do you suppose . . ."

"What?" Evie asked.

"I was just wondering if it was Tillie. She would have been on foot while her car was in the shop."

"Ask Gary if she waited in the shop the whole time."

"Okay."

Beth hovered her pencil over the page in her notebook. "I don't know what to put down about that. I guess I'll just write, 'Who was in Miss Archer's house just before and since her death, and why?' with some question marks." She wrote it down. "There may be other motives for murder in Miss Archer's past. Maybe something about her old boyfriend, Jack Cooper. I'll try to find out more from her friend in the African Violet Society and from Tillie."

"I notice that you haven't mentioned the Shakespeare books."

"I didn't want to say anything in front of Sandra, because Miss Tanner doesn't want that generally known."

"Yeah, I figured that was the reason. But now you should make a note," Evie said.

"Okay, I don't know what those books could have to do with her murder. But it is another odd thing." Beth wrote, "Shakespeare books" in her notebook.

"I should go with you when you visit Tillie."

"Why's that?"

"If she has something to hide, you shouldn't go alone. Even though I doubt that she had anything to do with Miss Archer's death. What would be her motive?"

"Sure. Come along. I welcome the company and the second pair of eyes. I agree that Tillie is an unlikely suspect, and I'm sure I could handle myself against an old lady if it came to that." Beth laughed.

"No doubt. Super librarian!" Evie laughed.

"We'll see if she was the mysterious visitor and, if so, the reason for her being there. So here's the plan. See Mrs. Schaffer at the hospital tomorrow and Tillie on Wednesday. And I'll check in with my brother to see if Tillie stayed in the shop during the repair or if she left," Beth said.

"Meanwhile, I'll show the photos of the painting around between classes," Evie said.

"And I'll check in with Mrs. Wren about the African violets." Beth glanced at the wilted plants on her kitchen counter.

Chapter 20

Tuesday, April 1

It was nearly seven o'clock when Beth and Evie met Sandra at the second-floor nurses' station.

"She seemed pretty lucid this afternoon. I hope she still is." Sandra led them down the hall to Mrs. Schaffer's room. "Remember, visiting hours end at eight," she said, and then left.

Evie took the chair next to the bed, and Beth stood behind her.

"How are you feeling?" Evie asked.

"Pretty good," Mrs. Schaffer said. "I don't know why they're keeping me here. I hope I can go home soon. Even if the nurses have been very nice to me."

"And the doctors?" Evie asked.

"Oh, you know how doctors are, always in a hurry." Mrs. Schaffer struggled to sit up.

"Here, let me help you." Evie jumped up and started arranging the pillows under her. "Comfy now?"

"Yes, that's fine. Thank you. It's nice of you girls to visit me." Mrs. Schaffer pushed herself up a bit more with her elbows and looked from one to the other. "I'm sorry, my eyesight isn't so good. Who did you say you were? You look familiar," she said to Beth.

"I'm Beth, and this is my friend Evie. I work in the library. I think we met there."

"Oh, yes, Beth," Mrs. Schaffer said. "My sister was named Beth—well, Elizabeth. We called her Betsy."

Beth decided to encourage this stroll down memory lane. "Oh, really? That's nice. Did you grow up in Davison City?"

"Oh, yes, I always lived here. That is, until I got married. I married a farmer, you know. We farmed outside of town for many years. After we retired, we moved back."

"Did you know Almira Archer when you were a girl?" Beth asked.

"Of course. Such a nice girl. Always running and playing. She grew up to be a school teacher, you know. That is, until . . ." Mrs. Schaffer trailed off, looking into the distance, a troubled look on her face. "And then something happened."

"Yes, she got polio. But before that," Beth said. "She had a boyfriend named Jack, didn't she? Do you remember Jack?"

"Jack? Oh no, not Almira. The other one." Mrs. Schaffer looked to Evie. "Was that Jack?"

"Was who Jack?" Evie asked.

"He came to see her, the other day. I think," Mrs. Schaffer said. "But it couldn't have been. That was a long time ago. She's in the next room, you know."

"You mean Almira is in the next room?" Evie asked.

"Yes, have you seen her?" Mrs. Schaffer asked.

"Not yet," Beth said. "Maybe we'll go there next. You said a man came to see her. Did you see who it was?"

A blank look came over Mrs. Schaffer's face. "What's that?"

"You said a man came to visit Almira. Who was it?" Beth asked.

"Oh, that was her nephew," Mrs. Schaffer said. "You know, that Melvin. His posture is very poor, don't you think? He should stand up straight."

Beth smiled. "Very true. Do you remember when you saw him?"

Mrs. Schaffer stared out in space again. "I haven't seen Jack for ages. It was odd, you know. She said vines were growing up the walls. But I don't think that's right. When do you think they will let me go home?"

"Soon, I hope," Evie said. She turned to Beth. "Maybe we should go. We don't want to tire you out, Mrs. Schaffer."

They said their goodbyes and left, and then went back to the nurses' station.

"How did it go?" Sandra asked.

"She seemed pretty coherent at first," Beth said. "Except for getting her timelines mixed up. One minute she's talking about something that happened recently, the next minute she's back in her childhood. Toward the end she was rambling, so we thought we should go."

"That's pretty typical," Sandra said. "By the way, I took a look at Miss Archer's chart. She was on digitalis for her heart."

"Is that a strong drug?" Evie asked.

"Oh, yes," Sandra said. "It has to be taken in the prescribed amounts or it can be dangerous."

"Was it given to her while she was in the hospital?" Beth asked.

"Yes," Sandra said. "But not in the pill form. Digoxin was administered in an IV drip when she first came in, under the doctor's supervision, to shock her heart back into beating correctly. It seemed to work pretty well, and it looked like she was going to recover. Like I said, she was sitting up and working on revising her will. But then she took a turn for the worse and died."

"Has anyone found the will?" Evie asked.

"No. I suppose someone took it out of the hospital and destroyed it," Sandra said.

"Probably her nephew," Evie said. "According to what Mrs. Schaffer says. But we'll never prove it. She's hardly a credible source, the poor thing."

Back at her apartment, Beth gasped when she saw the shattered flower pot and battered violet on her kitchen floor. It was obviously Chestnut's work, but he was nowhere in sight.

"Where are you, Chestnut, you naughty kitty?" Beth called.

"Hiding out is my guess," Evie said with a laugh. "He knows he was bad."

Beth sighed in exasperation. "Oh well, one down and five to go, I guess."

Evie started to pick up the pieces of the shattered clay pot and deposit them into the trash. "I apologize on Chestnut's behalf," she said. "I don't know why cats are so fascinated with knocking things down."

"Testing if gravity is still in force," Beth said. She stepped around the mess on the floor, filled the teakettle with water, and put it on the stove to boil. Then she got out a broom and dustpan and cleaned up the scattered soil.

Evie surveyed the situation. "You could put something around the flower pots so Chestnut can't get at them," she said.

"Like what?"

Evie looked around. "How about some of your bricks?"

"I suppose that would work. But what about my books?"

"Maybe it's time you got an actual bookcase," Evie said. "I'll look around the house and see if we have one in our basement or garage."

"That's okay, don't bother. I think my mom has one in the attic. I'll ask her," Beth said.

"If not, garage sale season is starting soon. Meanwhile, we can just put the books in that box." She pointed to the box on the kitchen table that the African violets had been in. "Come on, I'll give you a hand."

They packed up the paperbacks and then pushed the box into the corner of the living room. When the teakettle whistled, Beth took a break to brew a pot of tea. Then they took the bricks into the kitchen and built a low brick wall enclosing the remaining violets.

Chestnut stalked into the kitchen, twitching his tail nervously.

"There you are, you naughty kitty," Beth scolded. "But we've outsmarted you. Now you can't knock down any more plants."

Chestnut ignored her and rubbed up against Evie's legs, who reached down to pet him. "Don't be mad at me," she said, pretending to speak for Chestnut.

"I'm not mad, but you don't get a treat right now," Beth said.

They prepared mugs of tea, took them into the living room, and settled on either end of the couch. Chestnut investigated the box in the corner, climbed in on top of the books, and curled up for a nap.

"It looks like he found a new favorite spot," Evie said.

"Yeah," Beth sipped her tea, kicked off her shoes, and yawned. "I feel like a nap pretty soon myself."

"I guess it's getting late, and I have homework. I should go soon," Evie said, glancing at her wristwatch.

"I do too. But before you go, tell me what you thought of our chat with Mrs. Schaffer? Do you think she really saw Melvin at the hospital on the night that Miss Archer died?"

"I think she saw him, or somebody, or at least she thinks she did," Evie said.

"How should we proceed?" Beth said. "Do you think I should I contact Melvin and see if I can get him talking?"

"Maybe. How about calling him up and asking him for tax advice?" Evie said.

"That won't work," Beth said. "After our encounter at the fish fry, he'd be suspicious if I called him out of the blue and suggested a meeting. Maybe we can arrange to bump into him somewhere."

Evie sat up straight, suddenly more alert. "Speaking of fish fries, I have an idea. We can catch him at the Big Boy on Friday. According to my friend Gloria, who waitresses there, he rarely misses the Friday special—all-you-can-eat fish fry, with French fries and salad, for $1.99."

"I thought she was a waitress at Woolworth's," Beth said.

"She changed jobs for better pay and, usually, better tips," Evie said.

"I guess Melvin missed last Friday," Beth said. "He was at the church's fish fry."

"Because, for the same two bucks, he got a comparable meal *plus* a beverage and a cookie. He's always on the lookout for a bargain. Gloria says he always orders the same thing, asks for second helpings, and never tips. She hates it when he sits at one of the tables in her section."

"Never tips, huh? That sounds about right. Okay, we'll try to catch him there. And it sounds like a good deal. Want to go?" Beth said.

"Count me in," Evie said.

Beth snickered. "We'll reel him in. What time do you think we should go?"

"Gloria says he stops in after work. He works in the business office at the Ag school, and he gets to the Big Boy about four-thirty."

"Okay, we'll plan on showing up around a quarter-to-five, and see if we can corner him."

Chapter 21

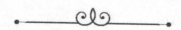

Wednesday, April 2

Beth struggled through the back door into her kitchen, lugging her book bag and two shopping bags containing potting soil, perlite, and African violet food that she'd picked up at the garden store in Grand Bend before heading home. She dumped everything on the table. She gasped, when she turned around and found tipped plants with bite marks on the leaves, spilled potting soil, and bits of chewed leaves scattered across her kitchen counter.

"Chestnut!" she called. "Where are you, you naughty kitty?"

He stalked into the kitchen, watching her, his back arched and tail erect. "Meow?" he asked.

"Meow, yourself. Did you do this?" Beth pointed to the damaged plants while Chestnut stared at the tip of her finger. She picked him up and pointed again. "Is this your doing?"

He pushed away from her, and she let him drop to the floor and skitter away under the kitchen table. Beth took off her winter coat, hung it on the hook behind the door, and kicked off her boots. Sighing, she righted the plants that had been tipped sideways behind the protective brick wall she and Evie had built the previous evening and started cleaning up.

"This doesn't bode well," she muttered.

Suddenly, a thought occurred to her. *Were African violets poisonous to cats?*

She crouched down to examine Chestnut, who had curled up against the wall, beyond her grasp, under the table.

"Are you feeling okay?" she asked. "I hope you don't have a tummy ache. I'd better call the African Violet Society lady and see what she says."

Beth consulted the white pages, found Mrs. Wren's number, and dialed it.

Mrs. Wren assured Beth that as far as she knew, no cat had ever been poisoned by eating African violet leaves. "By the way, our monthly meeting is this evening, seven o'clock, at the Lion's Club. Since you inherited Miss Archer's plants, or what's left of them, perhaps you'd like to join us? I can introduce you to some of our members and see if they have any experience keeping pets away from their plants."

Beth agreed to go. Then she pulled the box of Chestnut's food out of the cupboard and shook it enticingly.

"I'm not mad at you anymore. Come get your dinner," she said, as she poured it into his dish.

He slunk out, keeping an eye on her over his shoulder. Seeming to realize he was no longer in trouble, he settled down and crunched through his dinner.

Beth popped a TV dinner into the oven and pushed the bags containing gardening supplies to the back of the table.

"The repotting can wait," she told Chestnut. "I might pick up some ideas on the best way to do that at the meeting. On the other hand, if you continue to attack them, there might be nothing left to repot."

Beth called Evie and explained that she'd gotten an invitation to the African Violet Society meeting, postponing their trip to Tillie's house until tomorrow.

"That's fine," Evie said. "That will give me another day to investigate the painting."

It was a few minutes past seven when Beth parked in front of the Lion's Club, with its blue-and-yellow medallion over the door. Stepping into the lobby, she noticed an odor of dampness and stale cigarette smoke. It seemed that the faded green carpet could use a cleaning. A cardboard sign on an easel directed her to the room where the African Violet Society was meeting.

Beth walked into the dark-wood paneled room and saw small groups of middle-aged to elderly women, and a few men, standing behind the rows of metal folding chairs facing a podium set up at the back of the room, in animated conversation with one another.

Next to the door, a folding table was covered with small piles of leaflets and handouts. Feeling out of place, Beth occupied herself by examining the offerings. She selected one titled, "Best Practices for Repotting Your African Violets." The print and illustration on the mimeographed handout were a washed-out gray but were still readable.

"Are you finding what you need?" a voice behind her asked.

Beth turned to find the diminutive Mrs. Wren smiling up at her. Beth smiled back at her, surprised that she was the taller one. At only five feet four inches, that was an unusual situation for Beth.

"Yes, thank you." She displayed the handout. "I need to replant; the sooner, the better. Nothing on keeping cats away from plants, though."

"No, but that's a good suggestion for a future handout." Mrs. Wren laughed. "Meanwhile, I'll introduce you to Gerald. I believe he has cats."

Mrs. Wren trotted off toward two men who were engaged in a spirited exchange.

The taller one, with a gray fringe of hair around his shiny dome, was exhorting a shorter man with a bad toupee, who had turned a dark red and was clenching his fists. "I'm just telling you what works for me, an extra shot of fertilizer just before a show is best. I back off on regular feedings, and then—"

"Excuse me, Gerald and Jerry, sorry to interrupt, but I'm in a bit of a rush. This is Miss Beth Williams. Beth.

This distinguished gentleman is Mr. Gerald Fish," she said, indicating the taller of the two. "And this is his friend, Jerry Hollander."

They declared themselves pleased to meet her.

"Miss Williams has acquired a few African violets and has a cat who is overly interested in them. I was hoping one of you gentlemen might have a suggestion or two for her. Now, if you'll excuse me, I have to run off and make sure the microphone is working. We'll be starting the meeting in a few minutes."

"So you are cat lovers too," Beth said.

"I am," Gerald said. "But Jerry isn't. Just one of the things on which we differ."

"Mother would never allow a pet in the house," Jerry said.

"My mother is the same way," Beth said. "I never had a pet until recently, when I got my own apartment. So it's all new to me."

"By Mother, I meant Mrs. Hollander, my wife," Jerry said.

"Oh, sorry, I thought . . ." Beth trailed off.

"Not at all," Jerry said. "I call my wife *Mother*, a little pet name of mine. It does sometimes cause confusion. But no, I don't have a cat."

"I have two," Gerald said. "Midnight and Snowball. They are wonderful companions, but they can sometimes be annoying. Are you having a problem with your cat?"

"Yes," Beth said. "You see, I inherited Miss Archer's violets, and my cat, Chestnut, won't leave them alone. He wants to taste them and knock them over."

Gerald laughed indulgently, while Jerry scowled, seemingly scandalized at the thought.

"I don't have that problem, because I keep my plants in a spare bedroom, and the cats are not allowed in," Gerald said.

"And they are already in rough shape," Beth said. "The neighbor who took over watering them when Miss Archer got sick was overdoing it. I picked up some potting soil and perlite from the plant store today, and now I have this on repotting." Beth held up the handout.

"Did you also purchase some moss?" Jerry asked.

"Moss? No, the clerk at the garden store didn't say anything about moss. Is that something I need?"

Jerry and Gerald started another vigorous debate about the pluses and minuses of adding moss to the soil mixture. Soon, Mrs. Wren called the meeting to order.

Gerald hung back when Jerry left to find their seats. "Jerry doesn't know as much as he thinks. You'll be fine with just potting soil and perlite, as long as the plants get the right amount of light and fertilizer. I'll talk to you more after the meeting."

Then Gerald caught up with his friend, who had taken a seat in the front row.

Sitting in the back of the room, Beth let her mind wander during a nearly hour-long talk about new varieties of African violets and the rules for entering the upcoming regional competition in Fargo. This was followed by a round of spirited questions, several posed by Jerry. Then the meeting was adjourned, and Mrs. Wren invited everyone to stay for cookies and coffee, which she had set up on the table next to the door.

Being in the back row was an advantage. Beth had the best selection. She surveyed the offering and selected a chocolate chip cookie and fruit bar, probably rhubarb. Mrs. Wren appeared at her elbow as she poured a cup of coffee from the urn.

"Did you enjoy the talk?" she asked.

"Oh, yes, very much." Beth tried to sound sincere.

"In that case, I hope we can expect to see you at our future meetings," Mrs. Wren said.

Beth forced the smile to remain on her face. "I'm afraid that won't be possible, for the most part. You see, normally I work evenings at the library. This week is different due to the Easter holiday."

"Of course. Well, come when you can. You're always welcome."

Gerald appeared on her other side, as Mrs. Wren skittered off to chat with another member of the group.

"I've been thinking about your problem, and I think I might have a solution," he said as he beamed at her.

"Really, what is it?" she asked.

"I recalled that I had a terrarium in my garage. Well, it's just an old fish tank. I was going to make it into a terrarium, but I never got around to it. It's been sitting there for years. It's yours if you want it."

Beth said it sounded ideal and made arrangements to pick it up on Saturday morning.

"Wonderful," Gerald said. "One less thing in my way, and I'll be happy to have it put to good use. Miss Archer only had a few violets, compared to my collection, but she took great pride in them. She'd be pleased we're conspiring to try to save a few of them."

They headed back to the chairs, juggling cookies and Styrofoam cups of coffee, and found a spot to sit.

"Where's your friend Jerry? Has he left already?" Beth asked.

"Yes, he had to dash off. I'm afraid Mildred, that's his wife, keeps a rather tight rein on him," Gerald said. "She likes to imagine he's in constant danger of being swept away by another woman. In my opinion, that's a fairly unlikely prospect. It's not as though Jerry is a playboy, like our poor Miss Archer's boyfriend, Jack, was."

"Is that so." Beth said, turning toward him with renewed interest. "I take it you were acquainted with both of them when they were young?"

"Indeed I was." Gerald sucked a breath in through his teeth. "And what a dashing young man Jack was. He broke more than a few hearts in his time. Especially when he ran off and joined the fight in Europe."

"Wasn't he drafted?"

"Oh, no. He left before the draft began. Sometime in 1916, as I recall. Couldn't wait to get into the fight. All gung-ho. 'The war to end all wars,' and so on. Of course, now we know better."

"And he broke it off with Miss Archer by letter, while he was gone. Didn't he?"

"Yes. But how do you know that?" He scrutinized her face. "You seem very well-informed."

Beth felt her cheeks grow warm. "Miss Archer left her books to the library, and there were some papers mixed in with the books."

That was mostly true, she thought.

Mrs. Wren moved to the front of the room. "It was lovely to see everyone here this evening. But we have to get ready to lock up. If you would just dispose of your cups and things in the trash before you go."

Beth stood as she popped the last piece of rhubarb bar—she had guessed correctly—into her mouth and washed it down with a last sip of coffee.

"I'll see you on Saturday," she said. "Thanks again."

"Yes indeed, I look forward to continuing our conversation," Gerald said.

Chapter 22

Thursday, April 3

Beth drove north out of Davidson City while Evie scanned the sky and fiddled with the radio dial, searching for a weather report. This time of the year, anything could happen, from a blizzard to a thunderstorm to a perfectly lovely day. Today, the fading sun painted a slightly ominous picture of an overcast sky and blustery winds. The ditches were full, and fields were partially covered with meltwater.

"Nope, nothing on AM radio," Evie said as she switched it off. "We'll just have to keep an eye out for changing conditions."

"Should be okay; just cloudy this evening, according to the forecast. By the way, did you get a chance to show the photos of the painting to anyone?"

"I have big news about that. First, I showed it to a couple of art profs, which got me nowhere. They said they couldn't tell anything from a photograph. But then I visited the Art Restoration and Conservation store, and that was a lot more interesting."

"How so?" Beth asked.

"First of all, the owner said she still hadn't seen or heard from her assistant and is ready to fire her. She sent her a termination notice, and she asked me if I wanted the job."

"What did you say?"

"I asked if I could work around my class schedule. She said I could. So I said yes."

"Cool! When do you start?"

"Next week. It's just a couple of days a week, a few hours per day, at first. Then I'll see how it goes."

"I bet you'll like it a lot more than working at the sugar beet processing plant. And you can find out exactly when the painting was picked up and delivered back to Miss Archer's house. That may help us with the timeline."

"For sure. The question is, can I keep up with work and my coursework?"

"I doubt you'll have a problem. When we were in high school, you'd breeze through while hardly cracking a book while I slaved away," Beth glanced over at Evie. "Speaking of homework, sorry about dragging you out in the evening again."

"That's okay—no classes until Monday. There'll be plenty of time."

"Isn't it great? An actual long weekend! No classes, and the library is closed too."

"Yeah, it's great. And I'm looking forward to starting my new job, too. Except . . ." Evie trailed off and gazed out the side window.

"What's the problem?

"I have to come up with a painting I want to have restored. Remember, that was the story I used to approach them?"

"Oh, right." Beth laughed. "That's easy. Just say your mom changed her mind. Speaking of stories, what reason did you give for asking about the photo?"

"I racked my brain about that. I couldn't ask if the painting in the photo looked like a reproduction, because that might imply some skullduggery on their part. So I decided to ask about the frame."

"The frame? What about the frame?"

"I said I took the photo because I liked the frame on Miss Archer's painting and the frame on my mother's painting was damaged. I asked how much a similar one would cost."

"Brilliant! You're a natural detective."

"I'm getting there. And here's the big news—that question turned up a clue. She said that the frame on the painting in my photo was different. It was not the frame that was on Miss Archer's painting."

"What?" Beth oversteered to the right, almost running off the road as she stared at Evie, before slowing down and correcting. "She said what?"

"That the frame in the photo was not the frame that they put on the painting." Evie smiled at Beth's reaction. "She stared at the photo for a long time, and then said she was sure it was a new frame. That's weird, isn't it?"

"It sure is." Beth fell silent for a few moments, her forehead creased in thought. "That means either Miss Archer had the painting reframed after it was restored, which doesn't make sense. Why not have both things done at the same time? Or someone else took it and replaced the frame."

"Or it's a reproduction."

"Exactly. And if it is, who replaced it, and who has the original?"

"Which is why I swung by Miss Archer's sister's house after class this afternoon," Evie said. "I tried calling, but didn't get an answer, so I thought I'd drop by and see if she was home."

"You've been busy. Did you talk to her?"

"No, she was out shopping. But her husband was home. I told him I was an art student and I was interested in the artist, and he let me look at the painting. He was very willing. Almost eager, if you know what I mean."

"An aging Casanova?"

"Yup. While we looked at the painting, he tried to cozy up to me, while I kept edging away," Evie said. "I asked him about the frame. He confirmed that it was the original. According to him, his wife, Miss Archer, and their brother each got similar paintings from their dad, and he made identical picture frames for each of the paintings. Then I showed him the photo. He said he thought that the frame on Miss Archer's painting had been changed. But it had been years since he last looked at her painting, so he didn't know if it was a recent change or not.

Anyway, I had my camera with me, so I took a picture of the Petersons' painting."

"Okay. Good. On Friday we can show both pictures to Melvin and see which one matches his. Assuming he inherited his parent's painting and still has it."

"Right. That's one more thing we can ask him when we ambush him."

Beth turned into Tillie's driveway, bumped across the uneven surface, and stopped behind an unfamiliar car.

"It looks like she has company," Evie said. "Do you think we should go?"

"Not necessarily. Let's see what's what."

Beth parked and then grabbed the books she was planning to deliver to Tillie. They went into the porch and knocked on the kitchen door. Beth heard a low murmuring of voices coming from the parlor, and Buddy barked a couple of times. The door opened a few inches.

"Oh, hello," Tillie said, opening the door another few inches. Buddy stuck his nose out and sniffed, his tail waving. "I'm sorry, I can't invite you in right now. I have company."

"Who is it, Tillie?" A man's voice called out.

"Just some neighbor girls," Tillie said.

"That's okay. We just wanted to drop off these books for you," Beth said, holding them out. "There's an application for a library card too."

Tillie reluctantly took the books from her. "I don't have time to take care of that right now."

"That's okay. Just mail it in, or drop it off at the library the next time you're in town," Beth said. "Sorry to bother you."

"It's no bother. Do come again. I could go months between visitors, and now they arrive at the same time." Tillie laughed a loud, raucous laugh while closing the door.

Beth and Evie headed back to the car.

"Boy, she didn't want us to see who was there, did she?" Evie said.

"No, she sure didn't. I wonder who he is." Beth got a notebook and pencil out of her purse and wrote down the license plate and description of the car. "Let's see what we can find out."

Chapter 23

Friday, April 4

It was Good Friday, so Beth had been fasting. Now, she was looking forward to the one meatless meal of the day. Today that would be a fish dinner at the Big Boy. To have something warm in her stomach, she'd been drinking a lot of tea all day. As she alternately knelt and stood during the afternoon Stations of the Cross that had started at 3:00 p.m. at Our Lady of Sorrows Church, she was glad that Father McClure was speeding things along. She glanced at her watch. It was a quarter past three, and Stations would be wrapping up soon.

After the service concluded, she genuflected and turned to leave the church, when she spotted Mrs. Selvig sitting in the back row, glaring at her. Her expression changed to a simpering smile when their eyes met. Beth nodded as she passed and kept walking. She needed to nip downstairs to the ladies' room before heading out. Hopefully, Mrs. Selvig would be gone by the time she came back upstairs.

Beth took her time, but when she reentered the vestibule, Mrs. Selvig was there, scanning the notices on the bulletin board. There was no way out of the church without passing her.

Beth nodded to her again. "Hi, how are you?"

"Can't complain. I wonder if we could have a word?" Mrs. Selvig said.

"Now? I'm meeting someone soon," Beth said.

"This won't take long."

"Okay," Beth said. "What's on your mind?"

"I want you to stop stirring up trouble."

"Stirring up trouble? What do you mean?"

"You know perfectly well what I mean." Her eyes narrowed. "You're digging up the past. All that business about my daughter, and how she was hounded out of high school. As if our family hasn't suffered enough."

"I see," Beth said. "I wasn't aware that I was digging up anything, except in regards to Miss Archer."

"She was a bitter old maid, and now she's dead," Mrs. Selvig said. "Leave it alone."

Beth was shocked by the venom in Mrs. Selvig's voice. She glanced around and confirmed that they were alone. She chose her words carefully. "Miss Archer was my friend. I feel I should look into what caused her death. As far as I know, that has nothing to do with you or your daughter."

Mrs. Selvig blinked rapidly. "Everyone knows the cause of death was a heart attack."

"True. But what caused the heart attack?" Beth said. "I'm sorry for your trouble. It must have been an ordeal for your family. But that was a long time ago."

"It wasn't a long time ago for me or my family," Mrs. Selvig said, breathing rapidly. "It's still impacting us. Anna was expelled for no good reason. Miss Archer blew it way out of proportion. If she'd just looked the other way." Mrs. Selvig's face reddened as she spoke and her voice wavered. "Anna was so embarrassed that she left town for good. Now we only get an occasional phone call from her, and sometimes I wonder if she's alive or dead. We don't even know where she's living."

"I'm sorry," Beth repeated and began to walk past her.

"We still have some influence in this town," Mrs. Selvig said.

"What?" Beth stopped and turned back toward her.

"You heard me," Mrs. Selvig said. "If you value your job, tread carefully. A word to the right people from us is all it would take."

"Thanks, I'll keep that in mind," Beth said. She pushed open the heavy wooden door and walked out of the church, her legs shaking.

At home, Beth fed Chestnut and changed into her favorite bell-bottom jeans and chunky turtle-neck sweater before Evie picked her up. They drove out to the Big Boy restaurant on the northwest edge of town, parked, and waited, watching for

Melvin's car. Meanwhile, Beth told Evie about her conversation with Mrs. Selvig.

"She sounds kinda unhinged," Evie said. "Do you think she might have killed Miss Archer?"

Beth paused to consider the question. "I think she's angry enough. But I doubt she's the killer. She seems like the sort who gets other people to do her dirty work. Like trying to influence someone so I'm fired. Anyway, why would she suddenly decide to kill Miss Archer, after all these years?"

"I don't know. Maybe something happened recently that we don't know about. And another thing—how'd she know about our investigation? Unless . . ." Evie trailed off. "Is she part of your mom's craft circle?"

"I don't think so," Beth said. "Anyway, if she had been there, Mom wouldn't have talked about the cheating scandal. She knows it's a touchy subject. Maybe someone else, who *was* there, repeated what was said and it got back to Mrs. Selvig. You know how people in this town love to gossip."

"Probably the same in every town," Evie said. She pointed at a car pulling into the driveway. "Look. There's Melvin's car."

They watched while he parked his rusty old Pontiac as close as possible to the restaurant door and then went inside.

"Let's give him a few minutes to order, and then we'll join him," Beth said.

"What if we ask to join him and he says no?" Evie asked.

"We won't give him a chance—I'll just say 'mind if we join you' and slide right in. Follow my lead." Beth laughed. "Have you got the photos of the paintings with you?"

"Yup." Evie patted her purse. "Should we show them to him before we grill him on his whereabouts on the night Miss Archer died?"

"Definitely. I want to get him talking before he gets defensive and clams up," Beth said.

They walked into the restaurant and saw Gloria walking toward the kitchen.

"Is your favorite customer here?" Evie asked.

Gloria rolled her eyes with a small laugh. "Yup. Right over there." She nodded toward a booth in the back corner. They marched over.

When Melvin looked up, Beth said, "Mind if we join you?"

She slid in before he could object. Evie slid in next to her. They smiled at Melvin, who glared at them from the other side of the booth.

"You know my friend Evie don't you?" Beth said.

"I've seen her around." Melvin nodded toward her. "Why are you two here?"

Beth forced a friendly smile. "We came for dinner, of course. We saw you sitting all by yourself, and we thought you could use some company."

Melvin opened his mouth to protest but closed it again when Gloria came over with glasses of water for Beth and Evie and handed them menus.

"I don't need a menu. I'll have the special and a coffee," Beth said.

"Same here," Evie said. "But make it a Coke for me."

Gloria noted their orders and left, while Melvin continued to glare at Beth and Evie. Then he shrugged slightly, as though acknowledging it wasn't worth making a scene to get rid of them.

"Did you just get off work?" Evie asked him.

"No. It's a long weekend," he said, staring over her head.

"Oh, right. It's great to have a long weekend, isn't it? Of course, I've had plenty of extra time off, since I quit my job at the sugar beet plant."

"Is that right?" Melvin said, without interest.

"Yup," Evie said. "I'm going to college now—majoring in art."

"You don't say." Melvin stifled a yawn.

"Yes. I find it very fascinating. As a matter of fact, you could help me with an art question." Evie extracted the photos from her purse. "I took these photos of your aunts' paintings—the ones your grandfather gave them. He gave one to your father too, I believe. Take a look at these."

Melvin reluctantly took the photos and glanced at them. Then he sat up straighter, and his expression changed to one of interest as he examined them more closely.

"What do you want to know about them?" he asked.

"I have an interest in the artist. Charles Marion Russell, isn't it? Do you still have your father's painting?" Evie asked.

"Yes, I do. Not that it's any of your business. It's hanging in my living room, where it has always hung."

"That's wonderful," Evie gushed. "You must really love it. Russell's paintings are so lively, don't you think?"

"Uh-huh." Melvin stared at the photos and seemed lost in thought.

"I bet you've seen your aunts' paintings many times," Evie said.

"What? Oh, yeah. At least, Aunt Almira's. I don't see my Aunt Beulah very often. I don't remember the last time . . ." He trailed off, still staring at the photos.

"You seem lost in thought. Is there something odd about the pictures?" Evie asked.

He glared at her, his eyes narrowed in suspicion. "What are you trying to pull? Are these really their paintings?" He asked.

"Yes, these are photos of their paintings. Why? Is something wrong?" Evie said.

"This frame is wrong," Melvin pointed to the photo of the painting hanging in Miss Archer's study. "All three paintings had the same kind of frame. My grandfather made them. I've never seen this frame before. It's different than mine and Aunt Beulah's. That is, I think it is. Unless she had it reframed."

"Do you recall if your Aunt Almira's painting had the same frame as your painting the last time you saw it?" Evie asked.

"Yes. I'm sure it did. Aunt Almira was going to have her painting restored. It was getting a bit faded and dusty. But this isn't hers," he said, pointing to the photo again.

With a look of disgust, he handed the photos back to Evie. "What are you up to? What does this have to do with majoring in art? Is this part of your so-called investigation?"

"I just became curious when I saw this painting and noticed the newer-looking frame. You see, I went to the Art Restoration and Conservation store in Grand Bend, and I got a job there. I start next week."

Melvin looked confused and bored. "You don't say."

Just then the meal was served, and they spent some time passing around salt and ketchup and starting to eat. Beth was pleasantly surprised. The fish coating and fries were crispy, the fish was tender and flaky, and the little paper cup of coleslaw was tangy and tasty.

"You were asking about our investigation," Beth said, between bites. "We do have a question or two."

Melvin glared at her. "Like what?"

"Well, we talked to a few people who saw you around Miss Archer's house before and after she was hospitalized. And again later in the hospital near the time of her death. We wondered if you noticed anything out of the ordinary that might cast some light on things."

"You mean, you wonder if I put a pillow over her face or something, right?" He said. "Anyway, who are these people who you've been talking to? I suppose you mean her nosy neighbor, Charlene? She was always spying on Miss Archer."

"Is that how it seemed to you?" Beth said. "She might characterize it differently."

Melvin snorted in derision.

"According to Charlene, she was looking out for Miss Archer. She brought her the extra bottle of milk or a pound of butter when she needed it. In fact, Miss Archer called her when she started to feel poorly, and she was the one who called for an ambulance."

"Charlene should have called me!" Melvin's voice rose and his face reddened. "I'm the next of kin. I'm the one who was always there, year after year, helping Aunt Almira in every way possible."

Beth paused to give Melvin a chance to regain his composure. She signaled Gloria and requested a coffee refill.

Once his face resumed its usual pallor, Beth continued. "I'm sure you were a big help, and that she appreciated it. But wouldn't her sister be the next of kin?"

Melvin choked on a bit of fish and washed it down with ice water.

"Technically, yes. But they were not on good terms. They rarely saw each other," he said. "She wouldn't have even known that Aunt Almira was in the hospital if I hadn't called her. After I was finally contacted."

"Why didn't they get along?" Evie asked. She smiled at him, and leaned forward, encouraging his confidence.

His eyes narrowed a bit, but he continued, "Something to do with the past. Maybe the house. I gather Aunt Beulah wasn't happy that my grandparents left the family home to Aunt Almira. Almira was the oldest, and unmarried, so I suppose it made sense to them."

"And that way, it was kept in the family," Evie said. "Otherwise, the house would have had to be sold and the proceeds divided. But your Aunt Beulah didn't see it that way."

"Apparently not," he said.

"How about your dad? What did he think?" Evie asked.

"We never discussed it," Melvin said. "As far as I know, he didn't care. He had a house of his own. So does Aunt Beulah, as far as that goes."

"Speaking of wills, do you know Mrs. Schaffer?" Beth asked.

"Who? What?"

"A nice little old lady. She has—well, had—the hospital room next to your aunt's," Beth said.

"Nope, never met her," he said.

"Huh. Cause she knows you," Beth said. "She happened to mention that she saw you in the hallway outside of her room on the night Miss Archer died. Doesn't ring any bells?"

Melvin's face reddened in anger again, and he stared down at his plate. He poked at his fish for a few moments before answering.

"First of all, what I do or where I go is none of your business. I'm not guilty of anything, and you're not the police. Second, what does that have to do with a will? Or is that just another one of your fantasies?"

"Miss Archer was changing her will while she was in the hospital, and it went missing," Beth said.

Melvin scrutinized Beth, then said, "So it was a nurse who put you up to this."

"Is it true?" Beth asked.

"Maybe," he said. "Aunt Almira had mentioned wanting to update her will. I don't know why. I advised her to contact her attorney. I don't know if she did or not."

"So you didn't see a revised will?" Beth asked.

"No. And before you ask, I don't know what she wanted to change either," he said.

"Are you expecting an inheritance?" Beth asked.

Melvin laughed sardonically. "As one of her few living relatives, I would think so. But we never talked about it, and I don't really care. She can—I mean could—leave it all to charity as far as I'm concerned. That's not why I helped her out. She was family, that's all."

He seems to mean it, Beth thought.

"Can you think of anyone who might have wanted to harm your aunt?" Beth asked.

"Not a soul," he said. "She didn't have an enemy in the world. I think you're off the rails on this one."

Melvin quickly finished his meal without another word, and then left.

Gloria came back to the table. "He left without asking for seconds? That's unusual. But he didn't leave a tip, and that *is* usual. You must have really bugged him. What did you say? Maybe I can use it to get rid of him faster next time." She laughed.

"We were just asking him about his aunt. You know, the one who died recently," Evie said.

"Oh, sure, Miss Archer. She was my teacher, back in the day," Gloria said. "Nice lady. She didn't get out much after she retired."

"Did you know about the whole cheating scandal thing?" Beth asked.

"Oh, sure. I knew Anna Selvig too. What a stuck-up little thing she was. I hate to say it, but a lot of us kids were glad when she got booted out."

"Really?" Beth said. "So she was not the little misunderstood angel that her mother makes her out to be?"

"Ha! Far from it. Smoking, drinking, and making out with the boys under the bleachers at every game. But putting on airs like she was Miss Goody Two-Shoes to the teachers and parents. It was just a matter of time before she screwed up big-time. It's just too bad that Miss Archer was the one who caught her, you know. Oh well, I guess it's all water under the bridge now."

Beth and Evie turned down seconds and left, after leaving Gloria a generous tip.

Chapter 24

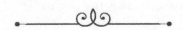

Saturday, April 5

Mr. Fish, or Gerald, as he said he preferred to be called, perched on a striped, straight-backed chair, stroking the long-haired white cat who snoozed on his lap. Beth sat facing him on the matching sofa and sipped excellent coffee from an eggshell-thin china cup. Gerald was explaining that this was his childhood home. His brothers and sisters had married and moved out of town, but he had stayed home and taken care of his mother after his father passed away.

While he talked, Beth admired the assortment of dainty china and crystal figurines displayed on doilies atop the fireplace mantelpiece and other surfaces. She carefully replaced her cup on its matching saucer on the coffee table.

"Gerald, how do you keep your cats from knocking over all your lovely ornaments? My cat loves to knock things down. He seems irresistibly drawn to my African violets," she said. "Knock wood, he may have lost interest. He's left them alone for the past couple of days."

"Oh, my cats are very well-behaved. Snowball wouldn't dream of doing such a thing. Would you?" he asked the sleeping cat. "Midnight can be a bit naughty. I felt very mean, but I was forced to resort to a few squirts with a plant-mister before he got the message." Gerald giggled.

Just as Beth had hoped, Gerald seemed eager to talk. When she came to pick up the terrarium, he'd loaded it into the trunk of her car and then invited her in for a visit. First, he'd given her the grand tour, including a glimpse inside of his greenhouse, a converted back porch with a stunning array of violets and other tropical houseplants soaking up the rays from the hanging fluorescent lights. She'd not been allowed to cross the threshold of the greenhouse. As he explained, a stray plant pathogen might have hitched a ride on her shoes or clothing. She didn't blame him. He'd obviously invested a lot into his plant collection and was justifiably protective of it.

Beth shifted on the uncomfortable couch and steered the conversation toward the olden days to see what more she could learn about Miss Archer and her family. "This morning I was glancing through a book that I checked out of the college library called *Prominent People of Davison City.* Are you familiar with it?"

"Yes, indeed. I have a copy of it around here somewhere," Gerald said, glancing around vaguely. "It is interesting, isn't it?"

"It really is. If I recall correctly, your family has lived in Davison City for many years. I believe they settled here around the end of the last century," Beth said.

"That's true. We came in the second wave after the railroad was built. The first few hardy pioneers came up the river, but many of them left after a particularly harsh winter. The cold, the isolation, and the difficulty of getting basic supplies proved to be too much for most people," Gerald said.

"I suppose it was a much smaller city when you were young," Beth said. "For example, the Archers had a much larger lot and then gradually sold off pieces of their property, and other houses were built around them."

"That's true. I must say, it's nice to see a young person with an interest in local history," Gerald's eyes lit up as he warmed to the subject. "As I said, the city really grew after the railroad came through. That made it easier for people to get here, bring in supplies, and buy and sell goods. My family saw the town develop from next to nothing. We were here when the streets were paved and the automobile took over from the horse and buggy. I saw the big bonanza farms come and go. Yes, I've seen it all."

"Oh, that must have been fascinating. I read about the bonanza farms. They were thousands of acres in size, weren't they? Imagine, farming so much land without gas-powered tractors, and harvesting it with just horses! And yet, they grew amazing amounts of wheat, which was shipped out by railcar. Wasn't it?"

"Yes, they used horses and also many, many temporary workers who arrived at harvest time. It was a boomtown, in those days. But the soil was depleted, and then . . ." Gerald drifted off and stared into the distance for a few moments. With a start, he shook his head and smiled. "Of course, now they have fertilizer and gas-powered farm equipment, so big farms are making a comeback." He waved a hand, dismissing the subject. "But you mentioned the Archers. Was there something in particular you wanted to know about them?"

"I admit, I do have a particular interest in the Archer family," Beth said. "You see, I was acquainted with Miss Archer for many years, since I first delivered library books to her when I was a high school library volunteer. But after she passed away, I discovered things about her that surprised me. I'm trying to fill in the missing pieces. I believe you and Miss Almira Archer were contemporaries."

"Yes, I grew up with the Archer kids," Gerald said. "It was a small town back then, so all the kids played together. I knew the Archers and Jack Cooper too."

"Ah, yes, Jack Cooper. Miss Archer's long-lost boyfriend. He went off to fight in the First World War, didn't he?" Beth said.

"He did. And the town lost a spark when he left." Gerald sighed. "He was one of those young men who created adventure everywhere he went. He raced around on horses, and later in cars. It didn't surprise me that he couldn't wait to get into the fight they called 'the war to end all wars.' He didn't want to miss out, I suppose."

"Do you recall how he started dating Miss Archer?" Beth asked.

"Well, that was surprising. A gaggle of girls followed Jack around, including the Archer girls and Maddie Selvig. He could have picked any of them, but he picked Almira. We were all sort of mystified."

"Maddie Selvig! Do you mean Anna's mother? Wasn't she quite a bit younger than Jack Cooper?" Beth said.

"Not as much as you might think. Maddie wears her age well. She's a few years older than her husband. And Anna was a turn-of-life baby," Gerald said. "She was a young teenager when she was hanging around with Jack and the rest of us kids. She had a big crush on him. All moon-eyed. You know what a first love can be like."

"That's so interesting," Beth said. "So when Miss Archer caught Anna Selvig cheating and Anna was expelled, Mrs. Selvig had more than one reason to be angry with Miss Archer, didn't she?"

Gerald nodded, knowingly. "I've always thought so. From Maddie's point of view, Almira stole Jack away from her. And later ruined her daughter's life."

"Why do you think Jack chose Almira?" Beth asked.

"It's a mystery. She was pretty, but not exceptional. Not as pretty as her sister, for example. But he was clearly in love. It may have been her wanderlust that attracted him."

"Because she was adventurous, like him?" Beth asked.

"Oh, yes. She talked about going out West when she grew up," Gerald said. "Her father spent some time roaming around before he settled down in Davison City, and he spun stories of his Western adventures. He grew sort of bitter about his lost youth over time."

"Bitter? Why was that?"

"I don't know. I suppose he expected more out of life. When you're young, you want fame and fortune, and then you find you've settled for raising a family and an ordinary life. I think Almira soaked up her craving for adventure from him. She wanted to live out her father's dreams," Gerald said.

"I suppose the Western-themed paintings he gave his children were part of that nostalgia," Beth said. "But she never did go west, did she? Do you think that's because of Jack?"

"Maybe. But also because she wanted to go to college first. Almira went to the Cities to get her degree," he said.

"Which was also pretty daring for a woman in her day," Beth said.

"Yes, it was. She was a modern girl. After she left, Jack was at loose ends, which probably contributed to his desire to get away and have an adventure of his own."

"And then Miss Archer caught polio while living in the Twin Cities, and Jack never returned from the war," Beth said.

"True. Almira was sick for some time. Her parents had to sell some of their land to pay for her care. And her sister went into nursing to help care for her. Once Almira was well enough, she finished her teaching degree, but she never fully recovered. She always walked with a limp. And, as you said, Jack never returned."

"So she gave up her dreams of Western adventure."

"Eventually. At first, she hoped to fully recover. But that hope faded over time," Gerald said.

"Do you think she was also waiting for Jack to return?"

"Perhaps. I think she was puzzled by his loss of interest, but was too proud to talk about it," Gerald said.

"It's such a sad story," Beth said.

They both sat and quietly thought about it.

"Well, I'd better get going. I promised my mother I would help her make pies for our Easter dinner."

With many thanks for the terrarium and the hospitality, Beth departed.

Later that day, Beth went to her parent's house. Her mom mixed ingredients, rolled out pie crusts, and put them into the oven to bake. Meanwhile, Beth stood in front of the stove. Her job was to stir the pudding mixture as it cooked. She'd finished the vanilla pudding and was now stirring the lemon pudding. Per tradition, her mom was making two of the family's favorite spring pies, lemon meringue and banana cream.

Her mom explained the steps she took as she went along. "As they say, this is as easy as pie. Now that you've done some cookie baking, maybe you're ready to try making a pie."

"I don't know," Beth said. "Between work and school, I don't have a lot of time. Maybe I'll give it a try this summer when I'm not taking classes."

As she stirred, she told her mom what Gerald had said that morning. She finished by saying, "So what do you think of what he said about Mrs. Selvig?"

"What about her?" her mom asked, looking up from the mixing bowl, holding an egg in one hand.

"That she blamed Almira Archer for stealing her boyfriend and ruining her daughter's life. Do you think that's true?" Beth said.

"Possibly," her mom said. She cracked the egg and poured it back and forth between the two half-shells, allowing the white to pour into the mixing bowl and depositing the yolk into a separate small bowl. "It seems unlikely she'd hold a grudge about a childish crush all these years. The thing with her daughter? Yeah, she probably holds a grudge for that."

"Enough of a grudge to want to harm her?" Beth asked. *Or harm someone who is investigating her death?* she thought.

"You mean, was she mad enough to kill her? I doubt it. Anyway, why now? No, I think if there was something fishy about Miss Archer's death, it was probably someone closer to home. Speaking of which, remember how I said I was meeting with my craft group and would try to steer the conversation toward Almira Archer and Jack Cooper?"

"Yes. Did it work?"

"Kind of."

"What did you find out?"

"Well, Mrs. Schuman, who works at the drug store, was there. Do you remember her?"

"Sure, I remember her. What did she say?"

"She said Melvin Archer picked up Miss Archer's last prescription. She was surprised because the prescription is usually delivered to her."

"That's interesting. What about Jack and Miss Archer? Did anyone say anything about them?"

"Not too much, I'm afraid. Just what's common knowledge; he left for the war, she got sick, and he never came back. It was a long time ago. Most of us didn't know Almira when she was young and never knew Jack at all. There was some speculation about why he never returned. Some thought he probably just fell in love with someone else. One of the older members of the group had known Jack when he was young. She said he hated to see disabled veterans, and would never want to live like that. She wondered if he couldn't face life with a disabled wife."

"That's interesting." Beth thought that over as she stared into the yellow pudding bubbling up around her spoon. "Or maybe Jack was injured in the war, and he thought Miss Archer felt the same way he did. So he broke it off to spare her from having to put up with a disabled spouse."

"Maybe. His sister might be able to tell you more about that."

Her mom came up behind Beth and peeked into the pan. "You'd better turn that down, dear. Just a slow boil. We don't want to scorch it."

"Okay," Beth said as she adjusted the burner. "You're right, I should try to talk to Tillie again."

Chapter 25

Friday, April 11

Beth and Evie sat next to the window in the cafeteria. Between work and classes, they'd only been able to talk on the phone this week. Beth filled Evie in on what she'd been doing since they last met and what she'd learned about Jack and Miss Archer's relationship.

"We should visit Tillie this afternoon. Are you busy?" Beth said.

"No, I'm not busy. That sounds like fun," Evie said.

Beth poked at her Tater Tots hot dish with her fork, took a small bite, and added salt and pepper. "How's your new job going?"

"It's interesting," Evie said. "I was pretty nervous, and the first day was kind of crazy. The owner just showed me around, handed me the keys, and took off. But the second day was better. So far it hasn't been busy. I think it'll work out great as a student job."

"Hah! She just turned over the keys and ran. She must have thought you looked trustworthy," Beth said.

"Or she was desperate enough to take a chance. She said she's been working nonstop ever since the previous employee disappeared, so she was in a rush to get home. I don't blame her. And she left a phone number and said to call if anything came up. But as I said, it was quiet. There were only a few customers each evening, so I have plenty of free time."

"It sounds like we might both get some extra free time next week," Beth said. "The river is supposed to crest any day now. If it gets any higher, they'll have to close the bridges, and we won't be able to get to the college."

"That's what they say." Evie nodded. "I wonder if the art restoration shop will close, or at least close early if that happens."

"Either that or the owner will have to cover a few more evenings on the job if you can't make it," Beth said, and then forked up a mouthful of hot dish.

"I suppose, but I hate to take time off so soon after I started," Evie said.

"Not your fault—act of God and all that. I'm sure your boss will understand."

"Yeah, I guess. Anyway, I wanted to tell you what I discovered while I was working. Some pretty interesting stuff," Evie said with a mysterious smile.

"Do tell." Beth laid down her fork and gave Evie her undivided attention.

"I looked into the delivery of Miss Archer's painting. It was delivered on March 16 by the former employee, Diana Flambois."

"Okay, so the date matches. We were in the house on the fifteenth, the night after Miss Archer died, and the painting was gone. Then they delivered it the next day. So it was back in place when we packed up the books the following week. Is that right?"

"That's right. But what we didn't know is that Diana Flambois is actually Anna Selvig."

"What?" Beth exclaimed. "You mean to say she's been in Grand Bend this whole time, living under an assumed identity?"

"I don't know how long she's been living in Grand Bend. But yes, she's been working under an assumed identity at the art shop for the past several months, according to her employment file."

"How is that possible? Wouldn't people recognize her? After all, Grand Bend is only twenty-some miles from Davison City, and we know that she made at least one delivery to Davison City."

"I don't know. Maybe she thought no one would recognize her. After all, it's been more than twenty years since she left home. And she's aged and dyed her hair black. But I recognized her, and I was just a kid when she disappeared. Maybe she doesn't care if she's found out."

"You recognized her? You mean you saw her?" Beth asked.

"Yeah. She stopped by yesterday. She said she was looking for her last paycheck. But I think she might have wanted to get her job back and expected to find her boss there. She seemed pretty surprised to see me there instead," Evie said.

"That's mind-blowing! Why didn't you call me and tell me?" Beth stuck out her lower lip.

Evie laughed. "Well, we were meeting for lunch today, and I wanted to see the look on your face when I told you. You were like this." She dropped her jaw and raised her eyebrows in an exaggerated look of surprise.

Beth laughed too. "You rat! So did she recognize you? Did you talk?"

"I don't think she recognized me, and I didn't let on that I recognized her. She was sort of glassy-eyed, like she was hungover or something. We only talked a little bit. I noticed some paint stains on her hands and asked her if she was a painter. She said she was, and I told her that I was an art student. That was about the extent of our conversation."

"This is a very interesting development. You know, Bill Crample stopped by the library the other day to tell me that they'd identified Anna Selvig's fingerprints on the frame of Miss Archer's painting. Apparently, Mrs. Selvig's darling little daughter was arrested at some point before she disappeared, so her fingerprints are on file."

"Yeah, and we wondered how on earth that could be. Now we know," Evie said.

Beth frowned. "Yup, now we know. Shoot! I thought it might be a significant clue. But I guess not. It makes sense that her fingerprints would be on the painting since she delivered it. Still, I bet Bill would like to talk to Anna—or Diana, as she now calls herself. Did you get her address and phone number when you looked at her file?"

"I did." Evie patted her book bag. "You can call Bill and fill him in."

"Or you can," Beth said.

"I could, but he's your friend," Evie said, smiling suggestively.

"He's not my friend. At least, not in the way you mean. We had one lousy date, and we both realized there was no chemistry," Beth said and shrugged. "But sure, I can call him. Give me the info."

Evie dug out her notebook, tore out the sheet with the phone number and address on it, and handed it to Beth. "I'll meet you in the Student Union around three this afternoon, and then we'll drive out to Tillie's. I can't wait to find out who her mysterious male visitor was."

"And what she was doing in Davison City on the day that Miss Archer got sick. Maybe she was the person Charlene Fleming saw leaving Miss Archer's house that day," Beth said.

Later that afternoon, Beth drove out of the college parking lot, through Grand Bend, and across the bridge into Minnesota. She slowed to a crawl as she drove through the shallow puddles of river water that covered the streets on both sides of the bridge. She glanced in her rearview mirror and confirmed that Evie was still following her as she drove out of East Grand Bend, and then turned north.

Beth uneasily scanned the surrounding area. Small patches of black earth dotted flat fields otherwise covered by water. The saturated ground had absorbed as much as it could, and the ditches alongside the roads were full.

Then Beth turned off the highway onto a gravel road dotted with puddles in low spots. Farmsteads stood as islands in a shallow sea, surrounded by sandbags and ditches. Beth remembered that this whole area was essentially a lake bottom. It had once been covered by a vast glacial lake, Lake Agassiz. It looked like it was trying to become one again.

They'd make it a short visit, she decided. If the overcast skies began to rain, it wouldn't take long to flood out what remained of dry land. At least her apartment and her parent's home were on what passed for higher ground on this prairie landscape. She'd feel a lot more comfortable once she got home.

They parked their cars in front of Tillie's house, in several inches of water, and splashed up to the front porch.

No point trying to keep my feet dry, Beth thought, looking enviously at the yellow rubber boots Evie was wearing.

"You should have worn boots," Evie said.

Beth gritted her teeth, holding back a "Thanks, Captain Obvious" tart response as she knocked on the door.

Inside, Buddy, the dog, was barking up a storm to announce their arrival. A few moments later, Tillie flung open the door.

"Come in, come in. But leave your wet things in the porch. I have enough trouble trying to keep the place dry with this one." She nodded at Buddy, who was joyfully sniffing around the girls, wagging his tail, and bouncing with excitement.

They stripped off their wet things. Beth took off both her shoes and socks, balancing as best she could while Buddy bumped against her, and then squished across the wooden floor into the kitchen with damp, bare feet.

"Sorry to drop in like this—" Beth started to say.

"Not at all," Tillie interjected. "What else could you do, since I don't have a phone? I suppose I should get one of those blasted contraptions—join the twentieth century before it's over—but I get along without it. Have a seat." She gestured at the kitchen table. "I was just going to put a kettle on for some tea. Can you stay for a cup?"

"Maybe a quick one. We should get home before it starts to rain. We didn't bring a boat," Beth said with a forced chuckle. "I just wanted to know how you liked the books I left you, and if you wanted to sign up for a library card."

"Well," Tillie hesitated. "Thank you for bringing those by, but you can return them. And I don't think I will get a library card. I don't get into town often, so borrowing library books wouldn't work for me. Anyway, I'd hate to have Buddy get hold of them and chew them up."

"Okay, I guess that makes sense," Beth said.

Tillie left the room, returned with the books, and put them on the table next to Beth.

"Did you find any new ideas for wild foods to try?" Beth asked.

"Well, maybe a few, but I mostly stick with what I know. There are wild plum trees in the yard and other fruits and berries I pick. I pretty much know what grows around here and what I like. Beyond that, I depend on what I can grow in my garden or buy at the store. I don't need much," Tillie said.

"Sure, I bet you could teach Euell Gibbons a thing or two," Beth said.

"It was interesting to browse through, though," Tillie said, examining Beth as though worried she might have offended her. "Thank you for thinking of me."

"No problem," Beth said. "As a librarian-in-training, I naturally try to get people interested in the library. But it's not right for everyone. You know, I used to deliver and pick up books from Miss Archer. I think she was a friend of yours."

"Oh? Well, I knew her of course," Tillie said.

"Then I'm sure you knew she had mobility issues. I started bringing her books when I was a library volunteer in high school," Beth said.

The teakettle whistled. Tillie jumped up and began preparing the tea.

"I wouldn't say we were friends," Tillie said. "But I've known her for many years, and I knew that she was lame from polio."

"So you weren't close?" Evie asked.

"No. She was more my brother's age. The older kids let me tag along sometimes. But I was one of the younger ones."

"You and Maddie Selvig," Beth said.

Tillie put the kettle down and turned to look at Beth. "Yes, like Maddie. But she was an O'Toole then, not a Selvig. How did you know about her?"

"I talked to Gerald Fish." She explained how they met. "He had an old terrarium he wasn't using and said I could have it. We chatted a bit about the old days when I picked it up."

"Huh, Gerald Fish. That takes me back." Tillie stared out of the kitchen window for a few moments. Then she picked up the teakettle, finished pouring hot water into the teapot, and brought it to the table. "I lost touch with that whole crowd after my brother left for the war. Like I said, they were mostly his friends. I guess he was the friendly one in the family. Then I got married and got busy with other things."

Tillie poured and passed out cups of tea and offered them honey and milk.

As Beth stirred in a generous dollop of honey, she said, "It's nice that you got a chance to see her one last time, on the day she got sick." Beth watched Tillie's reaction, hoping to gauge if she was the person Charlene had seen leaving the house that day.

Tillie nodded and then frowned. "I had some time to fill while my truck was in the shop, so I stopped by. I take it someone saw me."

"Yes, Miss Archer's neighbor noticed you leaving her house," Beth said.

"Figures. I don't miss having neighbors living close by. In town, there's always someone watching you."

"I guess that's true," Beth said.

Evie looked up from petting Buddy, who had snuggled up next to her. She said, "How did she seem? Was she okay when you saw her?"

Tillie seemed startled by the question. "Yes, fine. She was kind of surprised to see me. We talked about old times and tried to bury the hatchet."

"The hatchet? What hatchet was that?" Beth asked.

"Just a lot of nonsense. Water under the bridge." Tillie bit her lower lip, while Evie and Beth both looked at her encouragingly, hoping for more.

"Had there been a falling out?" Evie asked.

Tillie sighed. "It was all a big misunderstanding. I thought she broke off the engagement with my brother. But she said that wasn't the case. That he broke up with her. Well, he was in the war, and she was sick. Maybe some messages got lost. Or who knows what. Anyway, I'm glad I had a chance to talk to her. As it turned out, it was for the last time."

Tillie's face crumpled and she blinked rapidly. Buddy padded over to her and laid his head on her lap, looking up at her with big, sad eyes.

"Oh, you smelly old thing. You need a bath," Tillie said as she patted him on the head.

"By the way," Evie said, to change the subject, "when we stopped by to drop off the books the other day, it looked like you had another visitor. Did you have a nice visit?"

"Oh, that. Yes," Tillie said. She glanced out of the window. "It looks like it's starting to rain. You girls should probably get going while you still can."

They were soon on their way out of the door and sloshing back toward their cars.

"It seems like she didn't want to talk about her visitor," Evie said.

"I guess not. Do you want to come over to my place before you head home?" Beth asked. "I'd suggest stopping at the Big Boy for the fish dinner, but I don't want to sit there with wet feet. I can pop a couple of TV dinners in for both of us."

Evie laughed. "Tempting offer, but I think Mom is expecting me home for dinner. Talk to you tomorrow instead?"

Chapter 26

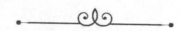

Saturday, April 12

Beth rolled the book cart full of returned books over to the adult fiction section. Before reshelving them, she paused to look out the window. Throughout the day, when she heard the repeated wails of the emergency sirens calling for more sandbaggers, she'd watched the progress of volunteers stacking sandbags around the bottom perimeter of the hill the library stood on. Now it was finished, and they had moved on.

Through the mist of a damp, gray afternoon, she watched the two men stationed on the bridge, a short block away. One wore a yellow slicker, the other a plaid wool jacket and a baseball cap. They held long wooden poles as they stared with fixed attention at the turbulent river water rushing toward them. The Rust Lake River was nearing a record flood level, and it flowed just a few feet below the bridge propelling blocks of ice, some as big as cars, toward it. Their job was to poke down the larger chunks of ice when they reached the bridge so they went under it rather than crashed into it. Pairs of men had been stationed there around the clock, on rotating shifts, and would remain there until the floodwaters subsided. As she watched, a newspaper reporter and photographer arrived to document their efforts.

Out of sight, to her left, floodwaters covered Central Park. Located in a hollow between the river and a railroad berm, the park often flooded in the spring. But this year, the river had spread further than normal. Gashes battered out of the river bank by floating trees and ice allowed water to pour out in spite of sandbagging efforts. Now floodwater covered the street running alongside the river, filled the outdoor swimming pool next door to the library, and lapped at the edges of a wall of sandbags that protected the library.

The library had been built almost fifty years ago and had never flooded. But this was a historic flood. As a precaution, high school library volunteers were working in the basement, removing reference books from the bottom shelves and piling them on tables. Beth heard a high-pitched squeal of laughter wafting up the staircase. She gritted her teeth, but then shrugged as she recalled being as young and carefree as they seemed to be. She only hoped that, as instructed, they were keeping the books in some sort of order, so it wouldn't be a huge job to reshelve them.

Beth started to turn away when a moving figure caught her eye. A girl was running along the riverbank. Her black, fringed coat swung over skinny legs encased in tight bell-bottom jeans. A long, red scarf unfurled behind her as she ran. Her dark hair swirled around her face. Beth watched as she leaped across one of the gaps in the riverbank and kept running toward the bridge. There was something familiar about the way she ran. A thought sprang to mind—*like the mad Ophelia*, remembering the character in *Hamlet* who drowned. She glanced at the group of men on the bridge. They were watching for ice and talking to the reporter and photographer, and they didn't appear to notice the girl.

The girl ran a few steps farther and leaped again, this time over a larger gap in the riverbank. Beth watched as she slipped sideways, arms flailing as she struggled to maintain her balance, and then slipped into the current of the raging river. She grabbed at the edge of the riverbank but lost her grip and was washed into the river and toward the bridge. There, she grabbed onto the bridge's undergirding.

"Oh, no!" Beth cried out. She jerked at the heavy oak window, rattled it, and then realized it was locked. She reached up, unlocked it, pulled it up, and called out, "Help her! Help her!" She pointed at the woman clinging to the edge of the bridge.

The men on the bridge looked vaguely in her direction. Beth realized they couldn't see the woman below them, struggling against the current.

Beth sprinted out of the library, down the front steps, and toward the bridge, yelling and gesturing as she ran. "Help her, help her!"

She splashed through the water, first ankle-deep and then knee-deep, as she neared the embankment. Water flew up until her pants were soaked. Using her hands too, she clambered up the slippery slope of the riverbank. Standing atop it, the water raged past only a few inches below.

By this time, the men on the bridge realized something was wrong and started running toward her.

Beth noticed that the young woman's red wool scarf had wrapped around her mouth, so she couldn't call out, and her eyes were wide open with terror. Her hands clung to the undergirding, knuckles white. Her feet had floated up as her body was sucked sideways and under the bridge.

Beth braced one foot against the concrete bridge piling and leaned forward.

"Grab my hand! Grab my hand!" she yelled. The woman tried. She loosened her grip with one hand and reached out. But the force of the current pulled against her, so she grabbed the undergirding even more tightly.

A huge block of ice collided with the middle of the bridge, shaking it. It splashed a wave of water over the young woman's head and washed up over Beth's legs. The current unfurled part of the red scarf. Beth braced her right foot more firmly against the bridge, leaned farther forward, and grasped the edge of the scarf.

"Grab onto your scarf," she cried out. "I'll pull you in."

The young woman, sputtering and gasping for breath, let go of the bridge with one hand and clung to the scarf, and then grabbed it with her other hand. As she clung to it, her body stretched out, like a bobber behind a moving boat. Beth hauled against the current, hand over hand, pulling her closer to shore.

The men from the top of the bridge ran up behind her.

"Here, let me." The man in the rain slicker grabbed the edge of the scarf.

The other man grabbed hold of Beth. "I've got you," he said.

She smelled the wet wool of his jacket as he put an arm around her and helped her off of the riverbank, back to standing in the knee-deep floodwaters.

"Thanks," Beth said. She noticed, for the first time, that the water was ice-cold, and she began to shiver.

The man in the wool jacket joined the other one, and they hauled the woman out of the water and onto the riverbank and then carried her up onto the bridge sidewalk.

Beth followed them. "Are you all right?" she asked the ashen-faced woman. She nodded, weakly.

"I work in the library," she told the men, pointing. "I'll go call an ambulance."

"Wait," The reporter said. "What's your name?"

Beth noticed the camera facing her and a flashbulb going off. *Had he been taking pictures of me this whole time?* She wondered as she patted at her hair. *I must be a mess.*

"Beth Williams. Now, I really must go and call that ambulance."

She turned and ran back through the murky floodwaters toward the library. When she entered, panting, she saw the teenage volunteers had gathered at the open window to watch the spectacle. They turned, open-mouthed, and gaped at her as she ran to the librarian's office to make the phone call.

Beth dialed 0 for the operator and told her, "A woman fell into the river. She was saved, but she needs medical attention. Send an ambulance to the Roberts Street Bridge."

Then she called Miss Tanner and briefly explained that she had to go home and change and why. At first, Miss Tanner seemed too stunned to form a complete sentence and merely sputtered. But after a bit more of an explanation, she said that was fine and that she would take over for the remainder of the afternoon. As Beth left the office, the heads of the girls, who had formed a circle in animated conversation, came up and gawked at her again, then mutely nodded as she told them that they were in charge until Miss Tanner got there.

The wail of the siren told Beth the ambulance was on the way as she slogged, dripping, to her car. Now she just wanted to get home and soak in a hot tub until she stopped shaking.

Beth let herself in the back door of her apartment as the phone on the kitchen wall started to ring. It continued to ring, insistently, as she dropped her purse on the floor and peeled off her coat, which was clinging to the damp legs of her pants.

"Let it ring," she announced to Chestnut, who sniffed at her sodden shoes and then marched off, back arched and tail erect in disapproval.

Beth picked up her purse, squished through the kitchen, and deposited it on the table. The phone continued to ring, and Beth reluctantly answered it.

"Beth? Is this Beth Williams?" the voice on the line asked.

"Yes. Who's this?"

"Dave Perry, from the Daily News."

She hesitated a moment, trying to place the name, "Who?"

"Dave Perry, a reporter for the Daily News. I just spoke to you a short time ago about the girl you pulled out of the river. I have a few more questions. Do you have five minutes?"

Beth sighed. "Can't it wait? I just came through the door and I'm soaking wet."

"Sorry, I'm on a deadline. I just need to verify a few things. It won't take long."

"Okay," she reluctantly agreed. "Five minutes."

He started to rapid-fire questions at her, most of which she answered with a yes or a no. Then he started asking about her background, where she grew up, her educational background, and her family. Finally, she interrupted him.

"Time's up. Sorry. I really need to go. Thanks for calling." She hung up as he started to ask another question.

Beth ignored the ringing phone while she drew a hot bath and sank into it. After a half-hour, clean and feeling restored, she wrapped up in her fuzzy blue bathrobe and slippers. She went back to the kitchen to feed Chestnut and make herself a sandwich. The phone rang again.

I bet it's that pesky reporter, she thought. *Won't he give up?*

She picked it up. "Yes?"

"Beth, is that you? This is Mr. Flack, from the newspaper."

"Oh, Mr. Flack. I'm sorry. I thought it was someone else."

He chuckled. "I bet you mean Dave Perry. He can be quite persistent. Comes with the job, I'm afraid."

"Yeah. He wouldn't stop asking questions. So I kind of hung up on him. Sorry."

"Don't be. Happens all the time. His story just landed on my desk, and I wanted to check in and see if you're okay."

"Yeah. I'm fine." Beth recalled the photos the news photographer was taking. "I'm glad you called. Can you do me a favor?"

"Sure thing. Unless you're going to ask me to kill the story. That I can't do," he said.

"Well, in that case, can you run it without a picture of me?"

He chuckled again. "Tell you what. I'll look for the best one. Good enough?"

"I guess so. Quid pro quo, can you tell me something?"

"If I can."

"Who was that girl, and how is she doing?"

"Now those are very interesting questions. Her name is Anna Selvig, and she's doing okay. They're keeping her in the hospital overnight. I gather she suffered some hypothermia."

"Not surprising. That water is freezing." Beth said. "Anna Selvig? The Selvigs' long-lost daughter?"

"Yup. One and the same."

"Oh, wow," Beth said. "What can you tell me about her? I gather she had some run-ins with the law before she left town."

"That's true. But how do you know that?" he said.

"I hear things," Beth said.

"I guess you do. I should hire you as an investigative reporter. Well, yes. Anna was a wild teenager. After she was expelled, she was arrested a few times. Nothing too serious, as I recall—petty shoplifting, underage drinking, that sort of thing. Then she took off for parts unknown. I believe that a few letters requesting money place her in San Francisco. But when they stopped dishing out the dough, the correspondence dried up."

"And now she's back," Beth said.

Beth suddenly realized why Anna had looked familiar when she saw her running on the riverbank. She was the woman who had knocked her over in her rush to get out of Miss Archer's house!

After a few more pleasantries, Beth hung up and immediately called Evie.

"Can you come over?" she asked. "I have a scoop for you."

"What is it? Tell me."

"Not until you get here. Turnabout is fair play. This time, I want to see the look on your face."

"Okay, I'll be right there."

Chapter 27

Saturday, April 12

Evie and Beth sat curled up on either end of Beth's couch, clutching mugs of tea. Chestnut was sleeping between them.

"You haven't made much progress reorganizing this room," Evie said. "I see your books are still in the box where we put them." She pointed to the box in the corner. "I guess you haven't gotten a bookshelf yet."

"I've been kind of busy. And I haven't decided if I'm going to move the African violets. They're doing okay on the kitchen counter. At least they're still alive, now that I have a terrarium to protect them from this one." Beth petted Chestnut, who raised one eyelid halfway and then closed it again.

Beth told Evie about the day's events and chuckled at Evie's reaction to how she helped pull Anna out of the river.

"My turn to surprise you," Beth concluded.

"Fair enough. I guess that makes you a hero," Evie said.

Beth laughed. "I wouldn't go that far. I just ran around yelling. Anna and I might have both drowned if the guys on top of the bridge hadn't come down to help us."

"And the newspaper reporter and photographer were there to immortalize it," Evie said.

"I suppose I'll get my fifteen minutes of fame. I just hope they bury it on an inside page. I hate to think about what I'll look like in the photo. I was a mess, all wet and muddy when I got home."

"I don't know, it sounds like front-page material to me. We don't get much excitement around here," Evie said.

Beth sighed. "I suppose it'll blow over quickly. There's always another news story coming along to capture everyone's attention. Anyway, get this—I realized when I saw Anna running along the riverbank that she's the girl who knocked me over when she ran out of Miss Archer's house."

"No way! Really? So that was Anna. When was that, the Sunday before Easter?"

"That's right."

"I wonder if that was when she swapped a reproduction for the real painting," Evie said.

"Hang on. Let me check my notes," Beth said.

She left the room and came back with her notebook and a pen. She flipped back and forth through its pages.

"Let's see, on March 15, the day after Miss Archer's death, we started to investigate. At that time, the painting was gone. Then Anna delivered the restored painting on the sixteenth. And it was still there on the twenty-fifth, when we were boxing up the books. Then, on the thirtieth—the day Anna rushed out of the house knocking me over—it looked like a different painting."

"Hang on," Evie said. "If Anna swapped the paintings, the real one must have been hidden somewhere in the house or taken out earlier. Because she wasn't carrying anything when she crashed into you, right?"

"I don't think so. I only caught a glimpse, but I think I would have noticed if she was carrying something as large as a painting," Beth said.

"And now Anna is back in town, and she was running along the riverbank. I wonder why she came back and why she was running, and why *there*," Evie said.

Beth stared into her mug for a few moments. "I'm just speculating, but what if she came back to see her parents and it didn't go well? She might have been running to blow off steam. Why she ran on the riverbank, I don't know."

"Or she could be just flakey," Evie said. "Think about it. She's kicked out of high school, gets arrested a few times, and then runs off to California. Years later, she comes back using an alias and gets a job at the art store. Then she disappeared from her job without any explanation, but she comes back later, maybe to ask for her job back. It kind of fits a pattern of her suddenly leaving and then coming back. You know—flakey?" Evie said.

"You might be right," Beth said. "If it's all part of a plan, I sure don't know what kind of plan it might be."

"Do you think she came back to get revenge on Miss Archer? If her life out in California started to fall apart, she might have obsessed over supposed past injustices and decided to blame her failures on Miss Archer."

"That's possible. Or she came back for some other reason; maybe she got homesick. She just happened to get a job in the art store, and when Miss Archer's painting came in, she hatched a plan on the spur of the moment."

"At any rate, she's a suspect."

"Oh yes, she's definitely a suspect. She had motive and opportunity. She came and went from the house at will, so she must have had a key. Either she was given one to make the delivery or she found one of the many spare keys that Miss Archer left lying around."

"On the other hand, the missing will points to a relative. Someone worried about being disinherited, either the sister or the nephew. As we now know, Melvin picked up Miss Archer's last prescription. He also was in and out of the house, frequently. So he also had opportunity and, possibly, a motive."

"Okay, so we have Anna, Mrs. Peterson, and Melvin." Beth jotted down the names. "What about Tillie? She admitted she was there on the day Miss Archer got sick and that she had some sort of a grudge against her."

"True. I suppose we should include her as a suspect, just to be thorough," Evie said. "But she doesn't seem the type. I thought she was telling the truth about wanting to bury the hatchet, and how she was glad she'd had one last chance to talk to Miss Archer."

"I agree." Beth scribbled in her notebook. "What would be her motive? She doesn't appear to have anything to gain. An old grudge over a broken engagement to her brother doesn't seem like reason enough to kill anybody. I'm putting a question mark next to her name. Anyone else?"

"Well, there's the Selvigs," Evie said. "Mr. Selvig lost his standing in town when his daughter was kicked out of school. And Mrs. Selvig had two reasons to hate Miss Archer: the expulsion, and Miss Archer stealing her would-be-boyfriend, Jack. No wonder she was so worked up when you bumped into her at church."

Beth looked up. "All true. However, where's their opportunity? As far as we know, they never had anything to do with Miss Archer."

"But they did show up at her funeral, which is kind of odd, when you think about it."

"Yeah. But Mrs. Selvig was a childhood friend of Miss Archer's. Maybe she just wanted to say her final goodbyes," Beth said. "Although, from the way she acted toward me, she doesn't exactly embrace forgive-and-forget."

"So what's our next step?"

"I think we need to go to the hospital and talk to Anna. I suppose she'll talk to me. After all, I did pull her out of the river," Beth said. "Shall we say, after church tomorrow?"

"Sounds good," Evie said.

Chapter 28

Sunday, April 13

Beth's phone rang first thing in the morning. Chestnut startled awake and raced across her. Cursing under her breath, Beth threw aside the comforter and raced into the kitchen to pick up the phone.

"Hello, yes," she answered, sleepily.

It was her dad. "Oh, hi, honey. I didn't wake you up, did I? I got the Sunday paper, and what a surprise, your picture is on the front page! The headline says, 'Heroic Librarian Saves Local Girl from Drowning.'"

Beth groaned. "Not really. I saw what was happening from a window in the library and ran over there without giving it a second thought. If I'd known my picture would be on the front page, I'd have let someone else pull her out of the river. As it was, the bridge guys did most of the work."

"Well, I'm proud of you. And most everyone else in town will be too. Except for your mother." He chuckled. "She's been fussing that you should be more careful."

He asked Beth if they should pick her up for church and, as usual, she said she preferred to get there on her own. Then he began reading the article to her and seemed prepared to read the whole thing. When he paused for a breath, Beth seized her chance to interrupt him.

"I just woke up, Daddy. I have to go. I'll see you later."

As soon as she hung up, the phone rang again. She considered letting it ring. But then she thought, *What if it's important*, so she picked it up.

A male voice said, "You don't know me, but I read about you in the newspaper—"

"Sorry, can't talk now," she said and hung up. Feeling unsettled, she turned down the ringer and ignored it while she got ready to face the day. Meanwhile, Chestnut followed her around meowing for his breakfast.

"At least you're acting normal," she said, as she got his food out of the cupboard and poured it into his bowl.

Later, when she entered the church, heads swiveled in her direction then bent together, and a buzz of conversation ensued. Beth lifted a hand in recognition to her family, sitting near the front of the church, but she took a seat farther back, next to Evie.

"Hi," Evie whispered. "I tried to call you this morning, but you didn't answer your phone."

"Sorry about that. The phone kept ringing, so I just ignored it," Beth whispered back. "What did you want?"

"I just wanted to see if your plans had changed. Are we still going to the hospital after mass?"

"Sure. In fact, let's sneak out after communion. I don't want to hang around answering questions," Beth whispered.

"Sounds good," Evie said.

Before the sermon, Father McClure prayed for those affected by the flooding, and then announced, "One of our parishioners was in the newspaper this morning. Perhaps you saw the story about Miss Williams and her brave actions to rescue a young woman. Not unlike the Good Samaritan." He led the congregation in a round of applause.

Wishing she could evaporate into thin air, Beth examined her hands as the heat rose in her cheeks. Finally, she looked up, nodded, and raised a hand in acknowledgment. That seemed to do the trick. The smattering of applause died out, ending the whole embarrassing episode.

After making good their escape, Beth and Evie arrived at the hospital and checked in at the nurses' station, where they found Sandra Brown on duty.

"Beth! I was just reading a story about you that's on the front page of the newspaper. Boy, I was surprised when I unfolded the morning newspaper and saw your picture."

"I haven't seen it yet," Beth said.

"You're kidding. Here, take a look." Sandra handed the newspaper to Beth. "Oh, and hi to you too, Evie."

The picture showed Beth from the side, pulling on a scarf, her right foot braced against the foundation of the bridge, with the raging river in the background. Beth passed it to Evie.

"Could be worse," Beth said. "At least they used a wide-angle shot. I was afraid my butt would be the focal point."

"No, it looks great," Evie said. "I feel honored just to stand next to the 'heroic librarian.'"

"Very funny," Beth laughed. "That's another thing—I'm not a librarian yet. Miss Tanner will be sure to point that out." Evie handed the paper back to her, and she scanned the article. "Other than that, it seems they got most of the details right. I suppose the reporter came to the hospital to interview Anna?"

"That's what I hear. I wasn't on duty last night," Sandra said.

"We're hoping we can see her. What's her room number?" Evie said.

"Oh, I'm sorry," Sandra said. "You just missed her. They kept her overnight for observation. But she must have been okay this morning. The doctor checked her over and discharged her. Her parents took her home."

"Bummer!" Beth said. "Well, maybe we can catch her at her parents' house."

Beth handed the newspaper back to Sandra, and she and Evie turned to go.

"Hang on a minute. I have some exciting news," Sandra said. "Well, not as exciting as rescuing someone from a river, but still interesting. We found Miss Archer's missing will."

"What? Where was it? Where is it now?" Beth and Evie both exclaimed, talking over each other.

Sandra glanced around to make sure no one was listening in on their conversation. "Remember Mrs. Schaffer, the little old lady with a room next to Miss Archer's?"

Beth and Evie nodded and said they did.

"We finally got her a bed in a nursing home. When the cleaners cleared out her room, they found it in her nightstand, which was full of all kinds of stuff. Apparently, she was wandering around when we weren't looking, latching onto things she saw lying around, and squirreling them away."

"Good grief! It's a good thing it didn't all get tossed," Beth said.

"For sure. Well, there were books, magazines, newspapers, and other stuff mixed in. The cleaners put it all into a laundry basket and turned it over to the nurses to sort out."

"Then what? What did you do with it?" Beth said.

"It wasn't me. I just heard about it later. The nurse on duty that day turned it over to Dr. Frost. He's making his rounds. He should be done soon if you want to wait."

"Should we wait?" Beth asked Evie.

"Of course."

They sat down in the waiting room and flipped through tattered back issues of magazines. Beth was just starting to read an article in *National Geographic* about a teenager sailing around the world alone when Dr. Frost hurried toward them. His graying hair was cut in a crew cut, his lab coat hung open over a gray suit, and a stethoscope hung around his neck. Beth was well acquainted with him and with his wife. They were both members of the Friends of the Library group.

"Miss Williams, Miss Hanson, how nice to see both of you. I saw in this morning's newspaper that you're a hero," he said to Beth.

She gave what was becoming her standard response that she was just at the right place at the right time and had only helped with the rescue. "But I suppose a heroic librarian makes a better news story," she said, with a self-deprecating laugh.

"I guess so. All the same, it was an admirable thing to do," he said. "I expect you came here to see Miss Selvig. Unfortunately, she's not here. But that's fortunate for her, in the sense that she was fine this morning. I let her parents take her home."

"So Sandra told us," Beth said, nodding toward the nurses' station. "I'm glad to hear she's doing so well. There was something else I want to talk to you about if you have a few moments."

"Of course. What can I help you with?"

"It's about Miss Archer's will."

"I see." He glanced at his watch. "I guess I can spare a few minutes. Come into my office."

They followed him behind the nurses' station into a small, cluttered room. His desk was stacked with files.

"Have a seat." He gestured at two wooden chairs facing the desk and sat down in a swivel chair behind it. "Beth, I understand you were a friend of Miss Archer's. I'm very sorry for your loss."

"Thank you. Yes, we were friends, although we only discussed books. But I was asked to look into her sudden death. I suppose because, as you know, I'd been involved in an earlier investigation." Dr. Frost had been present when Beth helped solve a previous case. "Were you aware that she had changed her will and the amended will was lost or misplaced?"

"Yes, I was aware of it. There's not a lot I can tell you about it. I signed it, if that's what you're wondering, but I didn't read the contents."

"Oh! I didn't realize that you had signed it," Beth said. "Was there another signatory?"

"Yes, one of the kitchen staff was collecting dishes and we pressed him into service. May I ask who asked you to look into her death?"

Beth hesitated, not wanting to cause trouble for Sandra, but she decided to be straightforward. "It was Sandra Brown.

You see, Miss Archer had asked her for writing supplies and to come back later to witness the will. But Sandra got busy and didn't get a chance to see her again that evening. When Miss Archer suddenly died, and the will was missing, Sandra thought it seemed suspicious."

"I see. It's too bad that she didn't ask me about it. Perhaps that would have allayed some of her concern."

"Possibly," Beth said. "However, it did take quite some time for the will to resurface. I understand it was turned over to you when it was found. Do you still have it?"

"No, I sent it to her lawyer, Mr. Nobis. As she had indicated that was what she planned to do with it. Was there anything else?" He glanced at his watch again.

"We don't want to keep you," Evie said. "But there was a question about something that Mrs. Schaffer said, right, Beth?"

Dr. Frost looked confused.

"That's right," Beth said. "Mrs. Shaffer was in the room next to Miss Archer's. When we talked to her, she said something about seeing a man in street clothes going into Miss Archer's room after visiting hours. She seemed to think it might have been her nephew. And of course, when the will vanished, it pointed toward a possible motive."

"But she was pretty confused at times when we talked to her. Remember how she said Miss Archer talked about vines that were growing up the walls of her room or something?" Beth asked Evie.

Dr. Frost had started sorting through files on his desk, but he paused and looked up with keen attention. "What's this? What did she say?" he asked.

"Mrs. Schaffer said Miss Archer said she saw vines growing up the walls of her hospital room. But she said she knew that couldn't be true," Beth said. "So although Mrs. Schaffer was a bit muddled at times, she was sharp enough to realize that vines don't grow up hospital room walls. So maybe she really did see someone in the hall who shouldn't have been there."

"I see, I see." Dr. Frost tapped his fingers on his desk. "You may be on to something. You'll have to excuse me now. I have to make some phone calls. I'll get back to you if anything comes of it."

Beth and Evie hurriedly said goodbye and left, while Dr. Frost searched through his Rolodex. They stopped outside his office to talk to Sandra.

"Dr. Frost asked me why I was looking into Miss Archer's death, and I told him it was because you had asked me to. I hope I didn't get you in trouble," Beth said.

Sandra glanced nervously toward Dr. Frost's closed office door. "I guess that's okay. He was bound to find out. What did he say?"

"Well, it was weird," Evie said. "He didn't seem very interested until we told him about what Mrs. Schaffer said, then he was suddenly eager to make some phone calls, and he said we might be on to something."

"Yeah, he did seem to suddenly take an interest," Beth said. "I don't know if he was just giving us the brush-off or what. Anyway, let us know if he says anything more about it to you."

Chapter 29

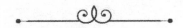

Sunday, April 13

Beth and Evie parked in front of the Selvigs' place, a multi-gabled wood and stone house, and walked up the curving sidewalk to a wraparound open porch. Beth rang the bell, waited, and then rang again.

High-heeled footsteps hurried to the door. It was cracked open, and Mrs. Selvig peeked out. When she saw who was there, she opened the door wider. She was wearing a Sunday dress and high heels. She smiled as she gestured for them to come in

"Come in, Beth, and . . ." she trailed off.

"Evie, Evie Hanson," Beth said.

"Oh, of course, Evie Hanson. I know you and your family, of course. Forgive me. It's been quite a day. Come in, won't you?"

After closing the door behind them, Mrs. Selvig paused in the foyer and turned to Beth. "I feel I should apologize for the way I behaved when we met in church."

You mean, when you ambushed me, Beth thought, but she just nodded and kept a polite smile on her face.

"I was overwrought," Mrs. Selvig said.

"That's understandable. Don't worry about it," Beth said.

Mrs. Selvig turned and led them into a dimly-lit living room. The closed drapes filtered the outside light. One floor lamp provided the only other light in the room. Mr. Selvig sat next to it in an overstuffed armchair and watched, over the top of his newspaper, as they entered.

"Dear, this is Beth and her friend Evie," Mrs. Selvig said.

He folded the paper, placed it on the end table next to his chair, struggled out of the chair, and came over to shake their hands.

"Nice to see you. Good of you to come. I suppose you came to talk to Anna. I was just reading about the events." He gestured in the direction of the folded paper. "Mrs. Selvig and I greatly appreciate your prompt action to help our daughter, Beth." A brief smile bristled his mustache and exposed the gap between his front teeth.

"You're very welcome," Beth said. "I'm glad I was at the right place at the right time. Yes, we would like to visit with Anna, if she's up to seeing company."

"She's in her room," Mrs. Selvig said. "She was napping. Worn out by the ordeal, I expect. I'll see if she's up." She clattered out of the room.

While she was gone, Mr. Selvig invited them to take a seat. Beth and Evie sat on opposite ends of the couch and made halting small talk about the weather. Mr. Selvig seemed on edge.

Probably to be expected, under the circumstances, Beth thought.

"I just heard on the radio that they are closing the bridges between Minnesota and North Dakota," he said.

"Really? I hadn't heard that yet" Evie said. "Did you?" she asked Beth.

"No, it must be a recent development," Beth said.

"I think so. I heard it just a short time ago," Mr. Selvig said.

"Well, I guess we won't be going to NDSC tomorrow," Evie said. "Did they say for how long?"

"They said they'd be closed for a day or two after the river crests, which is supposed to happen tomorrow," he said.

"I guess Anna will stay for a couple days then," Evie said. "Did she say what brought her back home?

Mr. Selvig eyed Evie suspiciously.

Beth bit her lip to keep from smiling. *Way to change the subject, Evie. We'll see where it leads.*

"No. We heard from her from time to time, naturally. But she didn't mention any plans to come home. Of course, we're glad she did," he said, unconvincingly.

"I'm sure you are," Evie said. "Only it was rather odd that she was living in Grand Bend for several months without letting you know, and using an alias. Don't you think?"

"She was doing what?" His mouth hung open, and the color rose in his face. "I, I, I . . . How do you know that?" he sputtered.

"I have her old job at the art store," Evie said, smiling disarmingly. She recounted how she'd gotten the job. "Then, one day, Anna came in looking for her last paycheck. She looked different, with dyed hair, and older, of course, but I recognized her. I have a good memory for faces. I wondered why she'd been working under a different name. Did she say?"

"No. That is, I haven't asked. That is to say, I didn't know . . ." he trailed off.

"It doesn't really matter," Evie said. "It's just sort of puzzling."

Mrs. Selvig clattered back into the room, followed silently by Anna. She wore a baggy, black T-shirt over bell-bottom jeans with frayed edges. Her heels hung over the backs of pink scuffs. An old pair of her mother's, Beth assumed. Her lank, black hair hung down to her shoulders, and bangs partially covered her sunken eyes.

"Look who came to see you," Mrs. Archer said to Anna, with forced cheerfulness. "It's Beth and her friend Evie."

Anna looked at them with disinterest that hardened into hostility. "You're that girl from the art store, aren't you," she said to Evie.

"Yes, that's right." Evie beamed. "And this is Beth. She's the person who saved your life, yesterday."

Anna snorted. "Right! Whatever." She walked over to a chair opposite the couch, kicked off her slippers, and curled her legs under her as she sat.

Beth had been quietly observing the family's interactions. Mr. Selvig hadn't said a word to his daughter. He just watched her with growing irritation. Mrs. Selvig glanced nervously between the two of them while maintaining a forced smile.

"Perhaps we should give the girls a chance to catch up," Mrs. Selvig said. "I hope you can stay for coffee. I was just going to start some."

Evie and Beth accepted her invitation.

"Dear, would you like to join me in the kitchen?" Mrs. Selvig said to her husband.

He seemed surprised by her suggestion, but he got up and said, "Yes, I guess I have some things I should attend to. It was nice to see you girls." He nodded goodbye.

"I could have saved myself, you know," Anna said after her parents left the room.

"Yeah, maybe," Beth said with a shrug. "I just acted on instinct. I saw you fall in and ran to help."

"Well, don't bother, next time," Anna said and pulled the afghan, which was behind her on the chair, around her shoulders.

"Okay. Next time you fall in the river, do it out of my sight," Beth said.

This caught Anna by surprise, and the corners of her mouth twitched up in a brief smile.

"So what's your bag?" Beth asked her.

"My bag?" The scowl returned. "What's that supposed to mean?"

"I mean you left town about twenty years ago, then reappear using an alias. What's that all about?"

Anna glared at her, eyes narrowed, for a moment. "Not that it's any of your business, but I reinvented myself when I moved to California. I was tired of being boring little Anna Selvig from Minnesota. I learned to paint and started using the name Diana Flambois. I just liked the sound of it. Anyway, I figured it would keep my parents from finding me. Not that they tried very hard. I guess they were glad to get rid of me."

I don't blame them, Beth thought. "And then you came back. Why?"

Anna shrugged. "I guess living out there got boring too. I figured I'd eventually meet up with some people that I used to know here and sort of start over. I'm kind of in transition."

"Another reinvention?" Evie asked.

Anna glared at her without a response.

"And why were you running along the riverbank?" Beth asked.

Anna glared at Beth, with narrowed eyes, for a moment, then closed her eyes and said in a low and intense voice. "I was exhilarated. Feeling at one with nature. Breaking free, like the river breaking free from the prison of ice."

Beth and Evie exchanged amused glances.

Anna opened her eyes, stared at them with an intense look, and said, "Know what I mean?"

Beth and Evie nodded and muttered agreement.

Mrs. Selvig returned carrying a tray full of cups, saucers, and a plate of cookies and other sweets, and deposited it all on the coffee table. She left the room again and reappeared with a carafe of coffee.

"Are you having a nice chat?" she asked.

"Oh, yes. Certainly," Beth and Evie murmured.

Anna just sat, wrapped in the afghan, and glowered.

Mrs. Selvig paused for a moment, as though wondering if she should join them. Then she said, "Well, help yourselves. I have to get dinner started." And she left the room again.

Anna unfolded herself from her chair, poured a cup of coffee, added several spoonfuls of sugar, stirred it in, and then retreated to her chair and wrapped her hands around the mug.

"Still cold?" Beth asked her.

"It's freezing in here. My parents hate to spend money on heating the house."

It must be nearly 80 degrees in here, Beth thought.

"So who are these people you were hoping to meet up with?" Beth asked.

Anna slurped some coffee. "Nobody in particular. Just kids from high school. I guess a lot of them left town."

"What was your graduating year? About 1949?" Beth asked.

"That's right. But I didn't graduate. Thanks to that old witch, Miss Archer." She glared at both of them, as though daring them to contradict her.

"I see." Beth poured a cup of coffee, passed it to Evie, and poured another one for herself. "Anyone want a cookie?"

She offered the tray around. Evie took a raisin oatmeal cookie, and Beth selected chocolate chip. Anna grabbed a handful of both kinds. Beth settled back on the sofa.

"What are your plans now?" Evie asked.

"You mean, now that you took my job?" Anna snapped.

"To be fair, I didn't so much take your job as you abandoned it and then they offered it to me."

Anna slurped coffee and gobbled cookies without answering. Evie looked at Beth and raised one eyebrow, her eyes dancing in amusement.

Anna finished the cookies and began brushing crumbs off her shirt and the afghan. "Maybe I'll take off and try someplace new—like Denver or Tucson. Anywhere has to be better than here."

"Interesting," Beth said. "Will you continue painting, do you think?"

Anna stopped brushing her crumbs. "Of course. I'm really good at it, you know. I've sold quite a few pieces," she said, animated for the first time.

"We'd love to see your work. Wouldn't we, Evie?"

"Of course," Evie gushed. "I'm studying art. I'm a beginner myself. But I'd love to see your paintings. When do you think we could do that?"

Anna looked guarded again. "I don't know. As I said, I might not be sticking around for long. I can't pay my rent without a job."

"Of course. Well, let us know what works out," Beth said. "We're often in Grand Bend, since we're NDSC students, and Evie works there now. Or are you planning to stay with your parents for a while?"

Anna snorted. "I am definitely not staying here. I'm going to go back to my apartment as soon as I can. I don't even have any clothes here." She poked at the slippers with her big toe. "Probably after dinner."

"Haven't you heard? The bridges are closed due to flooding," Beth said. "I guess you'll have to stay for a day or two."

"What? Really?" Anna said. "Damn, I should call . . ."

Mr. Selvig marched back into the room and pointed an accusing finger at Anna. "Is it true that you've been staying in Grand Bend for months without so much as a phone call?"

"Who told you that?" she said, and turned and glared at Evie.

"It sounds like you all have a lot to talk about. We should be going," Beth said. She put down her coffee cup and looked at Evie, who did the same. They left the room, found Mrs. Selvig in the kitchen, thanked her for the coffee and cookies, and said goodbye.

Once outside, Evie said, "Nice family. And what was that bit about Anna feeling "at one with nature?" I guess that's her idea of an artistic temperament."

They both laughed.

"Follow me. If we go around the side of the porch, we might hear the rest of this conversation." Beth gestured toward the side of the house.

They snuck around and stood near the closed window. They could hear angry voices. It sounded like Mrs. Selvig had joined her husband and daughter. The voices were muffled and faded in and out. Beth couldn't make out most of what they said. It seemed like the parents were pacing as they talked. Mrs. Selvig's voice was indistinct, just a rising and falling whine.

Suddenly, Mr. Selvig shouted. "Look what you've done to your mother." Later he yelled, "You're an embarrassment."

Anna shouted back, "Damn it! I wish I'd never come back to this godforsaken place." And then she started to sob.

There was a low murmur of voices, receding footsteps, and then silence.

After a few minutes, Evie whispered, "Should we go?"

They turned to leave, but the sound of a dialing phone stopped Beth. She held up a hand indicating for them to wait, and she put a finger to her lips. The phone must have been right inside the window. Anna's voice was clear.

Anna said, "Hello, it's me. . . . I can't get there tonight. The bridges are closed. . . . The flood, obviously. . . . No, I don't have it, but I can get it. . . . Tomorrow? Do you think you can make it? . . . Okay. Around midnight? . . . Do you have the money? . . . Okay. See you then." Beth heard the click as Anna hung up the phone.

Beth made a shushing sign again, and they tiptoed away from the window and off of the porch.

Back at her apartment, Beth prepared cheese sandwiches, chips, and tea. They took their lunch into the living room and sat on the couch. Chestnut settled, purring, between them.

"Are you going to call Bill?" Evie asked.

Beth pulled a face. "I don't know. Maybe he'd watch the Selvigs' place if he's on duty tomorrow night and doesn't have to go out on another call. But he can't just sit there. Even if he was willing, he'd be too obvious."

"What did you think of Anna?" Evie asked. "I bet she stole Miss Archer's painting. But does she seem like a killer?"

"Hard to say," Beth said. "She blames Miss Archer for her troubles, but no, she doesn't seem like a killer. Not that I know what a murderer seems like. What do you think?"

"Same here. She seems kind of flakey. Goes here and there on a whim. I suppose that's her idea of an artistic temperament. What's our next move?" Evie asked.

"A stakeout. Do you think you can come over before midnight tomorrow night?" Beth said.

"Sure, I'll just say I'm going out to meet some friends, and not to wait up," Evie said. "My parents don't keep close tabs on me anymore. How about if I come over around nineish?"

"Sounds good," Beth said. "We'll take my car. It's black, so it will be perfect for lurking."

Chapter 30

Monday Morning, April 14

Beth hadn't turned on the alarm this morning, since it was a day off from classes because of the bridge closures. She awakened slowly, opened one eye, and peeked at the clock. It was almost nine. She sat up, yawned, and stretched, waking Chestnut, who had been lying next to her, purring.

"Sorry, kitty," she said, as she slipped out of bed.

What luxury, she thought as she turned on the water taps and started to fill the tub for a soak. *I'll have a nice leisurely morning. Maybe catch up on some homework, housework, or do a couple loads of laundry.*

Her reverie was interrupted by a loud knocking on the front door. Swearing under her breath, she threw on her fuzzy bathrobe and padded barefoot to the door. Leaving on the chain lock, she opened it a crack. There stood Bill Crample, in uniform, staring off into the middle distance.

"Hang on," she said, closed the door, removed the chain lock, and reopened it. "Come on in," she said. "Wait a sec, I left the water running."

She dashed into the bathroom and turned off the water, noting there were only a couple inches in the tub. Fortunately, in this case, her water pressure wasn't great. She stuck her head back into the living room. Bill stood on the doormat, staring at his shoes.

"Can you wait for a few minutes?" she asked.

"I guess so," he said.

"Make yourself at home. I'll be right out."

Beth continued to swear under her breath as she slipped into jeans and a sweatshirt and ran a brush through her hair. Shoving her feet into a pair of scuffs, she reappeared moments later. Now Bill was sitting on the couch with his jacket unzipped. His hat rested on the cushion next to him. He was snapping his fingers and saying, "Here, kitty," trying to get Chestnut to come to him. Chestnut sat on the opposite side of the coffee table and eyed him.

"What brings you out so early?" she asked.

Bill looked at his watch, eyebrows raised. "Early? It's past nine."

Beth felt a prickle of irritation. "Yes, well, I took advantage of a rare chance to sleep in."

"Sure, sure," he said. "I'm sorry to disturb you. I suppose all the excitement around the rescue and the news story kind of took it out of you. Congratulations, by the way. That was very brave of you."

"No big deal," she said, embarrassed that he was being so nice after she'd snapped at him. "Come with me into the kitchen. I need to start some coffee and feed Chestnut."

Bill followed her into the kitchen, and Chestnut trailed behind him. At Beth's invitation, he took a seat at the kitchen table.

"Can you stay for coffee?" she asked. "It will only take a few minutes." Beth said as she prepared the percolator and plugged it in.

"No, thanks. I'm on duty. I just stopped by to relay a message from the Doc about Miss Archer. He wanted me to tell you that he's requested an exhumation and autopsy."

Beth was getting the cat food out of the cupboard. She paused, holding the box midair. "Really? When did this happen?"

"Recently, I guess. He just told me this morning."

"Did he say why?"

Bill crinkled his forehead. "Nope. Well, I guess he mentioned that something you said made him suspicious."

"Huh, something I said ... I can't imagine what that could be." Beth poured the cat food into Chestnut's bowl and returned the box to the cupboard.

"I guess you'll have to ask him about that," Bill said. He examined his hands folded on the tablecloth.

Beth began to feel annoyed with his inarticulateness. "You could have phoned to tell me that. Was there something else?"

He looked up, his eyes narrowed. "I understand you've been busy investigating."

"Is that what you *understand*?" she repeated, her voice dripping with sarcasm. "And what if I have? Obviously I was right about a few things. It seems like Dr. Frost also thinks there was something odd about Miss Archer's death. And it's pretty obvious to me that Anna Selvig is involved."

"Anna's involved? What do you mean?" he asked.

"Her fingerprints were on the painting," she said.

"I know. No surprise there. She was the one who delivered it," he said.

"And it's a reproduction. I thought you were going to interview her about it. Did you?"

"I don't know that it's a reproduction. And no, I haven't had a chance to talk to her yet."

"Well, I did."

"You did what?"

"I talked to her. Evie and I went to her parents' house yesterday and talked to Anna. We learned some pretty interesting stuff."

"Such as?"

"Such as that she's a painter. That's how she made a living out in California."

"I guess that's interesting," he said. "Of course, that doesn't mean she's an art forger, much less a murderer. Is that all?" he said.

"One more minor detail—she's planning to trade something for money at midnight tonight. My guess is that it's the real painting," Beth blurted out, and then immediately regretted it.

Bill stared at her with laser-like blue eyes. All hesitancy dropped, now he seemed like a cop grilling a suspect.

"She told you that?" he asked.

"Well, no, she didn't tell us. We sort of overheard it."

Beth turned her back to him and took her time preparing a mug of coffee.

"Are you sure you don't want a cup?" she asked, trying to sound casual.

"No, none for me. Thanks."

She took her mug and sat down across the table from him.

"How did you happen to overhear that?" he asked.

She lifted a hand and let it fall dismissively. "Anna got a phone call. We could only hear one side of the conversation, of course, but it was pretty clear what was going on."

"And she just spoke on the phone, revealing all this, while you were listening?" He narrowed his eyes at her.

"Not exactly."

"So what did happen? Exactly."

"Okay, we might have eavesdropped a bit."

She stared into her coffee, avoiding eye contact. After a few moments, she looked up. He was staring at her with pursed lips; his ice-blue eyes seemed to drill into hers.

"I see," he said. "I won't ask how that happened, because I don't want to know. But here's what's going to happen next. You're going to stay out of it. Got that?"

"Yes, but—"

"No buts! Just stay out of it. If there's anything to your story, which I doubt, leave it to me to follow up."

"The same way you followed up by interviewing Anna?"

He stood abruptly, his chair banged against the cupboards behind him, and he stalked out, slamming the door behind him.

Beth alternately laughed, swore, and paced, until she calmed down. Then she called Evie and updated her.

"So Dr. Frost asked for an autopsy," Evie said. "That's huge! Are you going to try to talk to him and find out why?"

"I can try to call him, but I assume he'll be busy with patients."

"What about Sandra Brown? Do you suppose he might have told her what's going on?"

"Unlikely, but possible."

"I'll see if I can get ahold of her. She might overhear something at the hospital. Anyway, what about our stakeout? Do you think we should call it off, after what Bill said?"

"No way. He'll probably blow it off. Like I told you, he doubted if there was anything to my story. Sometimes I feel like I could kick him where it hurts." Beth felt a flush of heat course through her.

Evie laughed and then said, "Okay, okay, take it easy. He's not the bad guy here. Just a little overprotective."

"Yeah, maybe. More likely just looking for reasons to do nothing. He had plenty of time to talk to Anna. But did he? No way!"

"That's true. I guess I'll see you later," Evie said and then hung up.

Chapter 31

Monday, April 14–Tuesday, April 15

Beth pulled the sleeve of her sweater down over her hand, stretched to reach the windshield, and rubbed a porthole onto the fogged-up glass.

"Crack your window," she said to Evie, while she rolled hers down a couple of inches. "I can't see a thing."

"Okay, but it's so humid out, I'm not sure that will help." Evie cracked open the passenger door window. "What time is it?"

Beth peered at her watch, but it was too dark. "I can't see, but it must be almost twelve. Anna will have to start out soon if she's going to meet someone at midnight."

They sat silently for several minutes, staring into the dark.

"Did you get hold of Dr. Frost?" Evie asked.

"Nope. I left messages, but he didn't get back to me. How about you? Did you talk to Sandra?"

"Yeah. She was totally surprised when I told her about the doctor's exhumation and autopsy request. That was the first she'd heard of it. She said she'd keep her ear to the ground," Evie said.

A rap on her car window made Beth jump. She turned and saw Bill Crample standing there.

"Come on. Get out," he said.

Beth rolled down the window, her heart beating out of her chest. She noticed that Bill was not in uniform. "What are you doing? You scared me half-to-death," she said.

"Get out of the car. Both of you," he said.

"Why? We're just sitting here minding our own business," Beth said.

"Do you want me to cause a ruckus? Cause I will. Then your little game would be over. So come along quietly."

"Okay, okay," Beth grumbled.

She rolled up the window and got out. Evie followed suit.

"This way." He led them to his pickup and opened the passenger door. "Get in," he said.

Evie climbed in first, and Beth followed. Bill climbed in on the driver's side.

"What's going on? You can't arrest us. We didn't do anything. Or are you kidnapping us?" Beth said.

Bill laughed and then said, "Actually, I suppose I could arrest you for loitering, but I'm not going to. And I am certainly not kidnapping you. Who would pay the ransom? And how much could I get for a mouthy little chick like you anyway? Nope, I'm helping you."

"Helping us? Why?" Beth asked.

"I knew you wouldn't stay out of it. So I'm keeping you out of trouble."

Beth thought about it for a few moments. "And I bet that some of the things I told you about Anna kind of sparked your interest."

"Maybe. We'll see. One thing's for sure—this truck has more clearance than your car," he said.

"What's that got to do with anything?" Beth asked.

"Did you ever stop to think that driving through puddles of water in the dark might not be the brightest thing to do? Your car might short out or float away."

"Pipe down, you two," Evie said. She pointed at the Selvigs' house. "Here she comes."

They watched as a car slowly backed out of the driveway into the street and then drove off. Bill put the truck into gear and followed, leaving plenty of space between the vehicles.

It was a quiet night. Monday nights generally were, but this one was quieter than usual. After driving several blocks, they hadn't seen any other cars on the road. Beth hoped Anna wouldn't notice them tailing her. So far, she was driving at a normal speed, which was a good sign.

A couple blocks later, Anna turned. Bill sped up until he reached the corner and then slowed down again after he turned. Within a few minutes, as they watched, Anna pulled up and stopped in front of Miss Archer's house. Bill parked further down the block.

"Back to the scene of the crime," Beth whispered.

Anna got out of the car. But instead of walking to Miss Archer's house, she turned and went next door to Charlene Fleming's house. She knocked, the door opened quickly, and she slipped inside.

"What's she doing?" Evie whispered. "Do you think Charlene is in on it?"

"Why are you whispering?" Beth whispered.

"Because you are," Evie whispered. Then she put her hand over her mouth to stifle a giggle.

"She can't hear us now," Beth said, speaking softly. "I suppose Charlene could be in on it. She has a key to Miss Archer's house. She probably got it for when she dropped off groceries."

"But didn't you see Anna run down the alley after she rushed out of Miss Archer's house?" Evie asked.

"I did. But she could have circled back," Beth said.

"Shh! Pay attention," Bill gestured toward the house.

They sat in silence and stared at the house as the minutes slowly ticked by. Beth watched as the mist turned into a steady drizzle. Finally, Anna reappeared with a painting-sized package under one arm. She put it into the back seat of her car, got in, and drove off.

They followed her for several more blocks, splashing through puddles in the intersections. She turned into an unlit, gravel parking lot between a grain elevator and the railroad tracks. She parked and turned off her headlights. Bill parked down the block and turned off his headlights.

Beth watched wavy patterns of rain forming and flowing down the windshield. "What do we do now?" she asked.

"We wait," Bill said.

A few tense minutes later, a dark sedan approached from the west and pulled in beside Anna.

"They're making the exchange," Beth said. "I can't see or hear a thing from here. Don't you need to go arrest them, or at least get closer?"

"Nope. We'll just wait and then follow the second car when it leaves."

"But Anna will get away," Beth said, with mounting agitation.

"I'll call for backup. There's a phone booth over there." He hooked a thumb over his shoulder, then got out of the truck and walked toward it.

"How long will that take?" Beth asked Evie.

"Who knows?" Evie said.

"Too long. They'll be gone by the time Bill gets back. I'm going to see what's going on."

"Shouldn't we wait?"

"You can wait if you want to. I'm going." Beth jumped out, closed the truck door as quietly as she could, and ran.

When Beth reached the worn, gravel surface surrounding the grain elevator, she tried to avoid the rain-filled potholes, but they were everywhere. *Damn! I just dried out these shoes. I really need to invest in a pair of rain boots,* she thought. Her socks squished inside her shoes as she edged around the building until the dark silhouettes of two cars against a shadowy background came into view.

She pressed up against the side of the building and watched as the driver of the second car opened his door, which turned on the dome light, and got out. He wore a tan rain coat. His face was shielded by a fedora. Beth thought he looked familiar, but she couldn't quite place him. He walked over to Anna's car.

When Anna got out of her car, she left the door open, providing a halo of light in the inky darkness. There were a few inaudible words between them. Then Anna opened the back door of her car, retrieved the package, and handed it to him. Beth heard the ripping of paper as he opened the edge of the package. He leaned toward the dome light inside Anna's car and pulled back the paper. Then he stood upright and nodded to Anna. He reached into a pocket in his raincoat, pulled out an envelope, handed it to her, and went back to his car with the package.

Just as I thought. It's all going to be over before Bill, or his backup, gets here, Beth thought. Her jaw clenched at the thought that they would get away.

The man placed the painting in the passenger seat and got in. As he turned to grab the door handle, Beth glimpsed his face. She gasped as she recognized him. It was John Peterson!

Beth flattened against the side of the building and turned her face down as the car headlights washed across the parking lot when the cars turned and drove away. As she headed back toward Bill's truck, it roared past her. She waved her arms, trying to get him to stop for her, but he didn't even slow down.

"Damn you, Bill Crample," she yelled at the receding taillights. Then she turned and saw Evie walking toward her, and she raised a hand in greeting.

"At least you didn't ditch me," she said when they met up.

Evie turned and started walking alongside her. "Yeah, well, I thought I'd better stay and see if you needed any help. Bill is following the second car."

Just then they heard the siren of a police car in the distance.

"I guess he got hold of some backup," Beth said. "Who do you suppose they're following, Anna or John Peterson?"

"John Peterson? Miss Archer's brother-in-law?"

"Yup, that's the one. I caught a glimpse of his face just before he left." It started to rain harder, and Beth picked up the pace. "Let's hurry back to our car. We're getting soaked."

After a ten-minute walk, they arrived back at the Selvigs' house. They got into Beth's car. All was quiet.

"I'll drop you off at your house," Beth said, between chattering teeth. "If anything was going to happen here, it'd be happening by now. Anna must have taken off in another direction, or they picked her up before she got home."

After dropping Evie off, Beth headed home. To her annoyance, she saw Bill Crample's pickup truck parked in front of her place. She ignored it, drove around the house, parked in her usual spot, and let herself in through the kitchen door. She kicked off her wet shoes and left them on the mat, hanging her dripping coat on a hook above it. Then she squished across the floor to the front door and opened it. Bill stood there, hand raised, about to knock.

He grinned at her. "You look like a half-drowned kitten."

Beth pushed back her wet hair. "I thought you were in hot pursuit."

"I was, but I decided to let the squad cars run him down. I got the license plate number, that's all I know for sure. He was headed toward Grand Bend."

"Yeah? Well, I know a lot more than that. I know who he *is*."

He gaped at her. "You do? Who is he?"

"John Peterson. He's married to Miss Archer's sister, Beulah. They live in Grand Bend."

"Are you sure?"

"Yeah, I'm sure. Evie and I met him when we went to their house to talk to Beulah. I don't know their exact address off the top of my head."

"That's okay. Close enough. Can I use your phone?"

"Sure." She let him in and pointed to the phone in the kitchen.

Chestnut sat on the couch, ears alert and eyes wide open, watching them. Then, startled by all the activity at this unusual hour, he jumped up and hid under the bookshelves. Beth plopped down where he'd been, peeled off her wet socks, and dropped them next to the coffee table.

Bill dialed the operator and asked for the Grand Bend Police. Beth went into the bathroom for a towel. When she returned to her spot on the couch, Bill was talking to the Grand Bend police. He identified himself, filled them in on what happened, and asked them to arrest Peterson and confiscate the painting.

He gave them a description of the car and the license plate number and then hung up.

He came back into the living room and stood looming over her.

"I want to talk to you about tonight—"

"Can we skip the lecture? I'm cold, wet, and bone-tired," Beth said, interrupting him, as she wrapped a towel around her head.

He hesitated, then continued, "Yeah, I guess so. I'll just say this—you endangered yourself needlessly tonight. You should have stayed out of it. Like I told you."

She sighed. "Got it. But I kind of saved the day, didn't I? I saw who was driving the car. If I hadn't, the painting might have been long gone by the time you got an ID on the license plate. "

He grimaced. "Well, I suppose I should thank you for that information." He hesitated again. "I guess I'll go," he said, and turned to leave.

"Bill?" she said as he opened the front door.

"What?"

"Thanks for trying to help," she said.

"No problem," he said.

"And let me know what happens. If they catch Anna and Mr. Peterson. Okay?"

"Yup. I'll probably talk to you tomorrow."

"Thanks," she yawned. "But not too early. I'm beat."

After he left, she locked the door and put on the chain lock. "You can come out now," she said to Chestnut. "Maybe I can get that soak in the tub I wanted this morning. Or was it yesterday morning? Whichever." She yawned again.

Chapter 32

Saturday, April 19

The din of voices rose from a murmur to a low roar as the room filled for the city council meeting. Beth scanned the room. Her family was there, of course. So were the parents of kids who came to the library for homework help, Friends of the Library members, and other folks from the community. Surprisingly, Bill Crample was there, in civilian clothes. Dave Perry, reporter for the *Daily News*, and the news photographer were also there. It looked like Miss Tanner's campaign to rouse the support of the community for the library had been a success.

Beth glanced at her watch; it was nearly ten o'clock. One by one, the mayor and the city councilmen started to move toward the front of the room and take their places on the dais. She was standing along the wall, greeting people, and thanking them for coming. Everyone seemed to want to stop and chat with her before taking their seats. They mentioned seeing her picture in the newspaper and thanked her for rescuing Anna Selvig from drowning. Beth was embarrassed by the attention, but she hoped it might help bolster the library's case. If the city council still intended to cut their budget and imperil her job, they had an uphill battle ahead of them.

One of the last two members of the Friends of the Library group to arrive was Dr. Frost.

"Thank you for coming, Doctor," she said. "I'm glad you were able to make it."

"Not at all." He chuckled. "My wife didn't give me much of a choice."

Beth laughed politely and murmured, "You and Mrs. Frost are such a big supporters. We very much appreciate it."

Beth spotted Mrs. Frost, president of the Friends group, hobnobbing with townspeople at the back of the room as they entered.

"But seriously, we both love the library," Dr. Frost said. "If our little city is to be considered more than a backwater, we must have a well-run library. You and Miss Tanner ensure that we do."

"I agree," Beth said, with a little self-deprecating laugh. "There is something unrelated that I want to ask you, if you have a moment."

"About Miss Archer's death, I presume," he said.

"Yes. I wondered if you could fill me in on that. According to Bill Crample, something I said to you made you suspect that she might not have died of natural causes."

"Well," he harrumphed. "Suspect is a strong word. It raised questions."

Beth glanced at her watch. They only had a few more minutes before the meeting would be gaveled to order. "Of course. Was there something in particular that raised questions?"

"Yes, there was." He glanced around as though seeking an escape from this conversation. "I suppose there's no harm in telling you that much. Although I must stress that it is not at all a definite thing. That is, we must wait for the results of the autopsy."

"I understand," Beth said.

"It was what Mrs. Schaffer said."

"Mrs. Schaffer?" Beth tried to recall what she'd said about Mrs. Schaffer, but she drew a blank.

"Yes, about vines growing up the wall. According to what she told you, Miss Archer had talked about vines growing up the walls of her hospital room."

"Yes," Beth said. "But that was just Mrs. Shaffer's dementia, I presume."

"Maybe so, but it made me wonder," Dr. Frost said. "Because those are the types of visual hallucinations suffered by someone who has overdosed on digitalis."

Beth stared at him open-mouthed. Just then, the mayor pounded his gavel, calling the meeting to order.

"We'll talk later," Dr. Frost said. He went to the back of the room to join his wife.

Beth took the seat the Miss Tanner had saved for her and listened as the sonorous voice of the mayor praised the people of Davison City for their response to the recent flooding.

"Thanks to the outpouring of help from members of the community, no lives were lost. However, there was significant damage to property, and it will take some time for everyone who was displaced to receive insurance payments and rebuild. The city will, of course, do what it can to facilitate the process."

He continued with an account of the damages and how the city would need to tighten its belt in the upcoming biennium to pay for the repairs. "In light of this, some of the less vital city services will have to be carefully considered."

As he droned on, Beth tried to sort out the implications of what Dr. Frost had just told her. *Melvin had picked up Miss Archer's last prescription, and that bottle of pills was still missing. Had he tampered with her pills? Was that why Miss Archer had had a heart attack? Mrs. Schaffer had said that she thought she'd seen Melvin in the hallway outside of her hospital room. He had been very cagey when they questioned him. Had he come back and finished her off? He probably had a motive. Without children of her own, Miss Archer may well have made him her heir. What if she'd changed her mind? Was that the change in her will that she was working on just before she died?*

But what did that have to do with the painting? It seemed like Miss Archer's death had something to do with the forged painting, and Anna and John Peterson had been arrested for that. They both denied any involvement with Miss Archer's death, of course.

And without any further evidence of involvement, they had been charged with theft and forgery. Maybe they were telling the truth. Maybe the forgery really had nothing to do with the murder.

While Beth pondered, people rose to support the library. Parents extolled the library's help in providing sources for their students' papers and helping them locate those sources. Mr. Flack, the newspaper editor, who was also a member of the Friends of the Library, talked at length about how much the resources had helped him in the book he was working on. And how Beth Williams had assisted him in his research.

There was a round of applause, and Miss Tanner nudged Beth and whispered, "That's for you. Stand up and acknowledge it."

Beth stood, nodded, smiled, and lifted a hand in thanks. A flashbulb went off, temporarily blinding her. When she could see again, she noticed the newspaper photographer a few feet away.

When she resumed her seat, Miss Tanner leaned over and whispered, "Try to pay attention."

Beth nodded, but she soon tuned out again as the meeting ground on. Finally, a motion was made, and seconded, to fully fund the library in the next budget. The *yea* vote was unanimous.

Miss Tanner turned to her, beaming. "Well done, Beth."

"Thanks, but I didn't really do anything."

"Nonsense," she said. "No false modesty, please. Your fame, fleeting though it may be, was the finger on the scale that saved the day. Now, if you'll excuse me." Miss Tanner left to mingle with the crowd.

Beth stayed where she was. Mr. Nobis slid into Miss Tanner's vacated seat. Beth thanked him for coming to the meeting to support the library.

"Of course. Our Miss Tanner made it clear that as a member of the Friends of the Library, I should attend. Is your friend Evie here today?" he said.

"No, she had to work."

"That's a shame. Such a lovely girl. How is she?"

Beth regarded him, skeptically. She had heard a rumor that Mr. Nobis's wife had gone for an extended "visit to her mother." The speculation was that she had tired of his roving eye.

"Evie is fine—still engaged to be married," she said.

"Of course," he paused and then changed the subject. "I noticed you talking to Dr. Frost."

"Yes," she said. "As you know, he is also a member of the Friends group."

"So he is. Did he happen to mention anything about the autopsy results?"

"He may have. Perhaps he would be better able to address that question."

"No doubt. It's just that my office is fielding questions about when we can probate the will. Normally, we would have done so already. But the latest developments have delayed it. I suppose he also mentioned the second will."

"I knew about it," Beth said.

"Did you know that you are one of the beneficiaries?"

"Me? Surely you mean the library. As you may know, we already have her books."

"No, I mean you specifically. Miss Archer left you a small bequest. You and several others," he said.

"Really? I had no idea. She never mentioned it, and I certainly wasn't expecting it," Beth paused. "I wonder—why was the library able to take possession of her books before the will was probated?"

He waved his hand. "They were not part of her estate. It's all documented. She'd intended them to go to the library before she died. But we never know when our time is up. Do we?"

"No, indeed." Beth said. "I hope that was not one of the things she modified in the handwritten will."

"The contents of wills are a matter of public record, once probated. Meanwhile, I can assure you that was not changed. But the holographic will could be another complication and delay."

"Holographic will? What is that?" Beth asked.

"That means a handwritten will. Even though it was properly signed and witnessed, one of the heirs may decide to contest the changes," he said.

Beth had an idea.

"What if you called all the heirs together for a preliminary reading of the will?" she asked.

"Why? What would be the purpose of that?" he asked.

"To answer questions about what is in the will and the probable timing of the distribution of assets."

He looked at her, one eyebrow cocked. "I have a feeling you have something more specific in mind. Okay, I'm game. What do you suggest?"

Beth explained her idea.

Chapter 33

Sunday, April 27

Beth placed one of the folding chairs, which she'd helped Mr. Nobis's secretary set up in the living room, facing the dining room so that when everyone was seated, they would be in her line of sight. They had arranged the chairs in an elongated circle, with a couple chairs behind the couch, closer to the front door.

As she took her seat, Beth reflected that Miss Archer's house seemed much the same as when she'd visited with her to chat about books. She almost expected Miss Archer to walk in at any moment. Only now everything was dusty, and her bookshelves were empty. And her African violets no longer bloomed in the dining room window.

They're still alive, and that's about the best I can say about them, she thought. *When I have more time, I'll try to get them to bloom again.*

The room was filling up. Mr. Nobis's letter promising information on Miss Archer's will had done the trick. At Beth's suggestion, he'd written that he didn't have an office large enough to accommodate everyone, so they would meet here, at Miss Archer's house. Beth hoped the location would evoke reactions from the assembly and get them closer to the truth.

After setting up the chairs, Mr. Nobis's secretary had gone home, declaring that he didn't pay her enough to claim any more of her weekend. Those in attendance, besides Beth and Mr. Nobis, included Miss Archer's sister, Beulah Peterson, and her nephew, Melvin Archer. Also there were Miss Archer's next-door neighbor, Charlene Fleming; Jack's sister, Tillie Damiere; nurse Sandra Brown, and Anna Selvig. Anna's presence was the most surprising. *Shouldn't she be in jail?* Beth wondered.

Once everyone was seated, Mr. Nobis took the floor. He welcomed them and thanked them for coming. Then he took a seat in one of Miss Archer's straight-backed, upholstered chairs, placed a folder on the end table next to it, and adjusted his reading glasses.

As he did so, an elderly man whom Beth didn't recognize slipped in through the front door, quietly closed it, and sat in a nearby chair. He wore a loosely cut, old-fashioned suit and a homburg hat pulled down over his face. Beth watched for reactions. Mr. Nobis glanced, almost imperceptibly, in his direction. No one else seemed to notice the new arrival.

"I want to reiterate, as stated in my letter, that this is not an official reading of the will. Due to circumstances, there will be a delay in the distribution of Miss Archer's estate. As her administrator, I will follow up with an official distribution letter once everything is settled. This is just an informal gathering to answer any questions that may arise," Mr. Nobis said.

"I am not aware of the circumstances," the new arrival said. His voice was well-modulated with a hint of a foreign accent. Beth noticed his high cheekbones and expressive, brown eyes. He must have been a real hunk when he was younger.

"Jack!" Tillie exclaimed. "I thought you weren't coming."

Beulah Peterson gasped and turned pale.

"I changed my mind. It's time I stopped hiding," he said to his sister. He stood, removed his hat and dropped it on the chair, smoothed back a full head of white hair, and then strode to the front of the room. "I am not aware of all of the circumstances," he repeated, standing in front of Mr. Nobis with clenched fists.

"Of course, Mr. Cooper," Mr. Nobis said in soothing tones. "Please have a seat; I'll explain what we know so far." Mr. Nobis indicated the couch. Anna Selvig reluctantly moved toward Charlene Fleming, and Jack sat down next to her in the vacated spot.

"For those of you who don't know him, this is Mr. Jack Cooper, Mrs. Tillie Damiere's brother," Mr. Nobis said. "I will recap the main points for his benefit, as well as to fill in any missing pieces for the rest of us. On March 13, Miss Archer fell ill and called her next-door neighbor, Miss Charlene Fleming, for help. Miss Fleming then called an ambulance, which took Miss Archer to the hospital, where she subsequently passed away. Her death was initially thought to be of natural causes."

"Initially?" Tillie asked. "But not now?"

"That is correct," Mr. Nobis said. "Miss Archer had suffered from an irregular heartbeat and was taking prescription medication. However, questions were raised due to a missing revision to her will, which she had been working on just before she passed away. That updated will was subsequently located and mailed to me."

Beth watched Beulah Peterson's face as Mr. Nobis spoke. She seemed to be in the grip of strong emotions. She alternately went pale and then red as she surreptitiously glanced at Jack. Her attention snapped back to Mr. Nobis at the mention of the altered will.

"That will is not valid. It was written by a sick, elderly woman who was no longer in her right mind," she said.

Mr. Nobis held up a hand and cut her off. "That is for a court to decide. There are . . . ," he harrumphed, "oddities, which will need to be sorted out. As I was saying, the missing will was located. But in the interim, her nurse, Sandra Brown, contacted Miss Beth Williams." He gestured toward them as he named them. "And she asked Miss Williams to look into the matter. Would you mind telling us why you did that, Sandra? Were you close to the deceased?"

"Me? No, I wouldn't say we were close. I knew her when she was a teacher, and I've seen her more recently as a nurse on several occasions. I guess I felt sorry for her, since she didn't have children of her own to look after her. Just a nephew." Sandra half-turned toward Melvin and smiled stiffly.

"And you thought there was something suspicious about her death?" Mr. Nobis prompted.

"Not exactly suspicious, but it seemed rather sudden. Miss Archer was getting better, and then she was gone. Of course, that is not unusual for someone of her age with a bad heart. But as you mentioned, there was the matter of the missing will," Sandra said.

"Tell us more about that," Mr. Nobis said.

"Miss Archer had asked me for writing supplies, which I gave her, and she asked me to come back later to witness a will when she was done writing it. I saw her working on it," Sandra said. "But then things got busy, my shift ended, and I went home. I figured I could witness it in the morning. But when I came back to work the next day, I was shocked to learn that she had died. Later, I was told that the will had disappeared."

"So you contacted Miss Williams," Mr. Nobis said. "Why not talk to Doctor Frost about it, or to the police?"

"I wasn't that sure," Sandra said, twisting her hands. "I just felt like if I hadn't been in such a rush to go home, maybe things would have turned out differently. But then I thought maybe I was overreacting or imagining things. I hoped if Beth looked into it, she would tell me there was nothing to worry about. Instead, the whole business with the painting started."

"The painting?" Jack asked. "What's this about a painting?"

Anna, who had been slouching on the couch, feigning disinterest, straightened up.

"Miss Archer had a valuable painting that had been given to her by her father," Beth said. "It went missing and was replaced with a forgery."

"Ah, yes, another one of those oddities that need to be sorted out," Mr. Nobis said. "I believe that Mr. Peterson is currently being detained in connection with an alleged forgery." He paused and scrutinized Anna and Charlene. Both of them looked very uncomfortable and avoided his gaze.

"I didn't know anything about it!" Charlene blurted out.

"Shut up, Charlene," Anna said.

"I won't shut up. I don't want anything to do with murder! Sure, I knew she'd nicked the painting." She cocked her head toward Anna. "She asked me to hide it at my place," Charlene said.

"How could you? Aunt Almira was your friend," Melvin said.

"Some friend. More like an errand girl. Get this. Do that. Always ordering me around like she was still the teacher and I was still her student. Anyway, I didn't know it was valuable or a gift from her father. It was just some dusty old picture of a guy on a horse. And it's not like she needed it anymore, did she? Why should her sister get it? She had little enough to do with her own sister while she was alive. That's what we figured. Right, Anna?"

"I told you to shut up," Anna growled.

"Why should I? And how come you're not in the slammer along with what's his name—Mr. Peterson?"

"Because I'm out on bail, stupid. What do you think?" Anna said.

Charlene slumped back against the couch, red-faced and fighting back tears. Anna clamped her jaw and stared at her hands.

Several people turned toward Mrs. Peterson, as though wondering why her husband had not gotten out on bail too. She tried to avoid their gaze. After a few moments of uncomfortable silence, she looked up and glared back.

"Why should I bail him out? So he can steal something else that belongs to me? He said he had long since swapped out my painting with a copy and that I'd never noticed it! So he thought he'd try it again. He met up with Anna Selvig, and they cooked up the scheme together. He always had an eye for any young woman. He said he wanted the money to leave me and start over. That he wanted to have some fun while he still could. I'm surprised they didn't run off together."

"As if!" Anna scoffed.

Mr. Nobis continued. "To get back to the will—"

"Wait. Before we get into that, I'd like to know more about Almira's death," Jack said. "Besides the will and the painting, is there anything else that indicates her death was suspicious?"

"I'm afraid so," Mr. Nobis said. "There was an autopsy. Preliminary results indicate that she was poisoned."

There were gasps and exclamations, and people talked over one another.

Mr. Nobis held up his hand. "One at a time, please."

"I don't understand. Why was an autopsy done?" Melvin asked. "I don't recall the doctor saying anything about needing an autopsy. He signed off on her death certificate, and she was buried. When did that change?"

"Only recently. Her body was disinterred, I'm afraid," Mr. Nobis said.

"But why?" Melvin asked.

"Some new information came to light, and the doctor decided it was best," Mr. Nobis said. "Apparently, some symptoms she exhibited may have indicated an overdose of her medication."

"An overdose? But how?" Sandra said. "Was there a mistake at the hospital, or . . ."

Beth scanned the room. Everyone seemed shocked by the news. "Or did it have something to do with the missing medication?" she asked.

All heads swiveled in her direction.

"What's this about missing medication?" Jack asked.

"Miss Archer's heart medicine went missing," Beth said. "At the time that my friend Evie Hanson—she helped me with the investigation—and I first checked out Miss Archer's house, she saw a bottle of heart medication in the medicine cabinet. Later, that bottle was missing. As far as I know, it is still missing. Unless someone here has found it."

Heads shook, and there were murmurs of no, as they looked at one another.

"Anna was in the house," Charlene said. "Maybe she took it."

Anna glared at Charlene. "You had a key too. Maybe it was you."

"Are you crazy? I just came in to water the plants," Charlene said. "Miss Archer would have wanted me to do that. I tried to take care of them, but they just didn't do well." She seemed close to tears again. "I tried to give them away. I asked her nephew and sister, but they didn't want them. Finally, Beth agreed to take them."

"Maybe that was part of the problem. Too many people watering them," Beth said. "They seemed kind of waterlogged. Who else had keys?"

"Well, I have a key," Melvin said. "But I didn't water the plants. You have one too. Right, Aunt Beulah? Did you water the plants?"

"I watered them once," Beulah said.

"You did?" Beth asked. "When was that?"

"I don't remember," Beulah said.

"I see. So several people had keys, and several people watered the plants. However, as I recall, her violets weren't doing great even before she passed away. I commented on it the last time we talked."

Melvin sighed. "She was trying out some new fertilizer after she couldn't get her usual brand. I think they stopped making it. I don't think she could read the fine print on the canister. She needed new reading glasses, but she had put it off."

"Enough about the stupid plants," Anna barked. "What about the pills?"

"Okay," Beth said. "Melvin picked up Miss Archer's last prescription not too long before her death. So there should be a nearly full bottle of pills around. Somebody took them. Perhaps the person who poisoned her. Was it you? Did you tamper with her pills, Melvin?"

"Me? How dare you!" Melvin turned bright red, strode across the room, and loomed over Beth, shaking a finger in her face. "You can't accuse me in front of everyone without a shred of evidence. You've been hounding me, asking me questions everywhere I go. I won't stand for it. Do you hear me?"

"That's enough," Mr. Nobis stood up. "Take your seat."

"But I, I, I . . ." Melvin sputtered.

"I said, sit down," Mr. Nobis commanded. "Now, if I may continue. I think the stipulations of the will, and its more recent amendments, might shed some light on things."

Melvin stalked back to his chair, sat down, and glared at Beth.

Mr. Nobis sat back down. "I'll skip all the legal mumbo jumbo. The gist of Miss Archer's most recent will, before her handwritten amendments, is that there are several small bequests of $1,000 each to Miss Williams, Miss Brown, and Miss Fleming, in appreciation for their kindness to her. She bequeathed Mrs. Tillie Damiere $2,000, in memory of her brother, Jack."

Beth blinked back tears at news of the unexpected gift. She noticed that Sandra and Tillie seemed similarly affected.

Charlene began to sob, excused herself, and ran into the kitchen. Soon, Beth heard the sound of water running in the kitchen sink. Then she heard the back door open and close. Apparently, Charlene had heard enough.

Mr. Nobis continued. "Miss Archer had intended that the remainder of her estate be divided between her sister, Beulah Peterson, and her nephew, Melvin Archer."

"Had intended?" Beulah asked.

Mr. Nobis looked at Mrs. Peterson, his face impassive. "Yes; according to a phone conversation with Miss Archer (witnessed by my secretary, incidentally), as well as her handwritten will, which was correctly dated, signed, and witnessed, she wanted to make some changes." He extracted a handwritten piece of paper, readjusted his reading glasses, and scanned the document. "The $2,000 bequest to Mrs. Tillie Damiere, in memory of her brother, was removed."

"I asked her to remove that," Tillie said. "Obviously, my brother is alive and well."

"And you knew this all along," Beulah said, bitterly.

"I asked her to keep it a secret," Jack said.

"You did?" Beulah's voice shook. "But why? After we heard you were missing in action, we all waited and wondered for years if you would ever return. Eventually, we assumed you were dead."

"That's a long time ago. I don't really want to talk about it. At the time, I wished I *had* died. I saw so many of my friends die in that futile war." Jack took a deep, ragged breath. "The truth is, I deserted."

There was a collective gasp.

"You went AWOL," Tillie corrected him. "If you hadn't gotten sick . . ."

He waved away her explanation. "Who knows what might have happened. The fact is, I did get sick, and then I met someone. We married, and I stayed in France. I was always afraid of what would happen if the truth came out. I'd face a court martial. Then prison, or worse. Many men were shot for desertion. So I just tried to forget the past and become another Frenchman. I couldn't let my family worry and wonder, so I wrote to them, but I asked them to keep it a secret. Now that my wife has passed away and our children are grown, I yearned to see my childhood home once again."

"You could have written to Miss Archer too," Beth said. "She would have kept your secret. Instead, you left her in limbo, never knowing if you'd return. Why?"

He turned to Beth and smiled sadly. "I did finally write to her, just recently. I asked if I could come and see her. Unfortunately, by the time I received her response and came home, it was too late. You see, for many years I thought that she'd broken up with me. Her letters were returned to me, marked "refused." And Beulah wrote that Almira had gone away with another man."

All heads swiveled to Beulah.

"She was sick," Beulah said. "She was recovering from polio. I was nursing her, and I didn't want her bothered." She wrapped her arms around herself.

Beth watched her, and missing pieces started to drop into place. *What was it that she'd been told? All the girls were half in love with Jack.*

"And you were jealous, weren't you?" Beth said to Mrs. Peterson. She paused. "But you didn't return all the letters, did you? I saw one letter from Jack saying goodbye and telling her that he intended to stay in France."

Beulah smirked. "I steamed it open. It didn't mention the returned letters, or my letter to him. And it was vague enough for her to think that he had ended it. I was happy to let her see *that* letter."

"You wanted Jack for yourself. That's why you sent back his letters, and you wrote those lies about your sister," Beth said.

"What of it?" Beulah cried out. "She always got everything she wanted! She got Jack, even though I was prettier than her, and she didn't really love him. If she had, she wouldn't have left him behind to go to college. And then she got sick. Well, it was her fault she picked up polio in the Twin Cities. She didn't have to go there in the first place! Meanwhile, I had to stay home, learn nursing, and care for her. Our parents had to sell off pieces of their property to pay for her education and her health care, and she still got the house after they died. What did I get?"

"You have a husband and a home of your own," Beth said. "She didn't."

Beulah laughed bitterly. "Some husband! A thief and a philanderer."

Jack look at Beulah with disgust. "You were always a selfish thing, weren't you? You always wanted *more*. Nothing was ever good enough for you."

The color rose in Beulah's face and she began to tremble, but she didn't answer him.

"That's right, you were a nurse, weren't you," Beth said.

Mr. Nobis harrumphed. "Shall we return to the business at hand? Other changes Miss Archer indicated in her handwritten will include a bequest of one thousand dollars to Anna Selvig."

Anna gaped at him. "She left me a thousand dollars? Why?"

"In her own words," Mr. Nobis read from the document, "I realized, belatedly, that I could have handled the instances of cheating in my classroom with more discretion. By following the letter of the law, I inflicted unanticipated harm on Miss Anna Selvig and her family. I hope this small bequest and a sincere apology helps her with her future endeavors."

Anna sat open-mouthed, staring at him as he continued.

"In addition to a small bequest to the Davison City branch of the African Violet Society, one notable change is that Miss Archer leaves her Charles Marion Russell painting to Mr. Jack Cooper. Again, in her words, 'To remember how much I loved him. And in hopes that he may still have a chance to explore the West, as we had planned to do together so many years ago.'"

There was a general sniffling and blinking back of tears.

"And, finally," Mr. Nobis continued, "I bequeath our childhood home to my sister, Beulah Peterson. I forgive her for her misguided actions all those years ago. I hope Jack can also forgive her. In spite of the deep pain inflicted on us, she is still my sister and I wish her only the best. The remainder of my estate goes to my nephew, Melvin Archer."

Beulah went pale and then started to laugh hysterically. Then she fell silent and rocked back and forth in her chair.

"What have you done, Beulah?" Jack asked.

"What do you mean? I didn't do anything," Beulah said.

"No?" Beth asked. "You had a key and went into the house to water the plants. That must have been after your sister was in the hospital. You were a nurse. You would know her pills could be used to prepare an overdose."

"What of it? I had no motive," Beulah said. "And she would have known it was me. How could I have administered an overdose?"

"I didn't think you had a motive. I wondered why an old feud over a boyfriend would suddenly result in murder. But it was because he was coming back. Wasn't it? You were afraid your interference and lies would finally come to light, and you wanted to prevent that," Beth said.

"But I didn't even know he was still alive, much less that he was returning," Beulah said.

"I think you did. Tillie must have told you," Beth said.

Beth turned to Tillie. "To 'bury the hatchet' is the way you put it. You'd resented Miss Archer for hurting your brother, but then you found out that she hadn't broken off the engagement. Between what Jack wrote and what you knew, the two of you must have worked out what really happened."

"That's right," Tillie nodded. "I brought along some of my special tea blend, and we had a nice chat."

Turning back to Beulah, Beth continued, "And then what? Did your sister call you and say she knew what you'd done?"

Beulah stared straight ahead. "She'd gotten a letter from Jack. He said he was coming to see her. Almira started to ask me a lot of questions, and I couldn't have the truth coming out. Don't you see? I suspected she was sitting on a pile of money. After all, she had a free house and never spent much. I was sure she would cut me out of her will if she knew the truth. And then, like a miracle, it seemed like everything would be okay. She had another heart attack. The hospital called me to let me know."

Beulah fell silent and rocked back and forth again.

"But you were afraid she'd recover, like those other times. So you made sure she didn't," Beth said. "You went into her hospital room, knowing her eyesight was bad, and administered the overdose."

Beulah looked around at everyone staring at her. Her eyes blazed with anger.

"She forgives me! She forgives me?" Beulah's voice rose to a screech. "Well, I don't forgive her! She took my boyfriend, my youth, and my chance at happiness. Yes, it's true. I killed her!"

The onlookers shrank back in horror.

"My nurse's training came in handy when I ground up and dissolved some of her pills and then injected it into her. It's funny; if you put on a nurse's uniform you become invisible in a hospital. No one suspected a thing. Until you started snooping around, you nosy girl." She turned to Beth. "Oh yes, I was the one who came back for those pills you're so curious about, and I disposed of them. I realized someone might wonder why so many of them were missing."

"Thank you, Beulah," Mr. Nobis said, in a soothing tone. "Let's all settle down now."

He nodded discreetly to Beth. She went to the front door, opened it, and signaled to Officer Crample, who was sitting in his squad car outside the house.

Chapter 34

Sunday, April 27

Beth and Evie sat on the couch and swirled wine in Beth's new wine glasses while they rehashed the events of the past couple of months. Chestnut slept between them.

"It's nice that you can afford luxury items like wine and real wine glasses to drink it out of, now that you're an heiress," Evie said.

Beth laughed. "I'm spending money I don't have! But I guess I feel wealthy enough to afford a few amenities, like these glasses."

"And your new roasting pan," Evie said. "That chicken parmesan smells incredible."

"I hope it's good. I got the recipe from my grandma. It involves a lot of fussy-business. So I probably won't make it too often. Thanks for being my guinea pig."

"I'm honored that you invited me to your premiere attempt. And I'm glad you're expanding your cooking attempts beyond peanut butter sandwiches and burned TV dinners."

Beth laughed. "I splashed out and got an oven timer too. No more burning anything. Knock wood. Of course, it'll be months and months until Miss Archer's will is probated and I actually get any of the money. *If* I get it. There's a lot to sort out."

"It sounds like it. Anna Selvig and John Peterson were charged in the theft of the painting, and I suppose Charlene Fleming was too," Evie said.

"Charlene probably won't get in too much trouble. She says she was just helping out a friend, and it's her first offense. We'll see what becomes of Anna. I hear she's back in her apartment in Grand Bend."

"Yes. Did I tell you? She came into the store for some painting supplies."

"No kidding? How did she seem?"

"She was in a good mood—even smiled a little. She said she got a job in a community theater working on props, and she's painting too," Evie said. "What about Mr. Peterson? Is he still in jail?"

"No, his lawyer sprung him. Now he gets to have all the fun he wants. He's on his own, since Beulah is in jail."

"Do you think she'll be convicted of murder?"

"Probably. She confessed in front of a bunch of witnesses."

"That must have been a shock to everyone. When did you begin to suspect her?"

"I wasn't sure until that day. As you know, we'd considered her as a suspect. But we thought an old grudge about a boyfriend didn't seem to be much of a motive for murder. And why now? After all these years? Then I saw how she reacted to Jack's arrival. She went all pale and even shook at one point. It seemed more than just being surprised. She seemed afraid. So I asked myself why, and it all started to fall into place. How she resented her sister. She had nurse's training, so she would know how to prepare an overdose. And she admitted having a key to Miss Archer's house, when we were talking about who watered the plants. The clincher was when I heard about how she interfered and lied to break off Jack and Miss Archer's engagement. I realized she didn't want that getting out. She was afraid of being cut out of Miss Archer's will."

"Let me see if I have this straight: when Tillie visited Miss Archer, they talked everything over, and Miss Archer started to guess what had happened," Evie said. "Then she called Beulah, asked questions, and told her Jack was alive and well and on his way home. That's when Beulah started to get desperate. Right?"

"Yup. It's too bad you couldn't have been there. You were as much a part of this investigation as I was. I never would have solved it without your help," Beth said. "But Mr. Nobis insisted that only people who were mentioned in the will should be there. I'm just amazed that I was one of them."

"That doesn't surprise me. After all, you were her friend. I'm more amazed by her bequest to Anna." Evie reached for another cracker topped with cheese.

"I was too. But then I thought about it, and it made more sense. Miss Archer must have been elated to learn that Jack was alive and coming to see her. So she was in an expansive mood when she was writing out that revised will—forgiving old wrongs and trying to mend fences."

"That sounds about right," Evie said. "It's just a shame that Beulah did what she did."

"I know. Talk about holding grudges! Beulah must have fantasized about how wonderful her life would have been if she'd married Jack Cooper instead of John Peterson, and she blamed her sister for preventing that. Personally, I don't think Jack would have picked Beulah, even if Almira was out of the picture."

"I guess we'll never know," Evie said. "Anyway, he doesn't sound like much of a catch. He volunteered to fight in the war, but he deserted when the going got tough. Then he left Miss Archer hanging and ran off with someone else."

Beth shrugged. "That was a brutal war. I guess I'll cut him some slack. A lot of guys broke down, got shell shock or whatever. It was too bad about Miss Archer. But he thought she'd dumped him. So when he met someone else, he decided to get on with his life."

"I guess so," Evie said. "From what they show on the TV news, war is hell."

"True. I hope televising it will put an end to the romantic notions that have led so many young men to volunteer." Beth popped another grape into her mouth.

Evie fell silent and stared into the middle distance.

"Are you thinking about Jim?" Beth asked. "What do you hear from him?"

"He writes often. But it takes a while to get his letters from Vietnam, so I never know if he's still okay or not. I can't wait until he comes home." Evie sighed.

Another woman left behind to wait and hope, Beth thought.

"I'm sure he'll be fine," Beth said. "Jim is a survivor."

"I know." Evie shook her head, as though to clear it. "Let's talk about something else. What about Miss Archer's house? Who gets it? Not Beulah, I assume," Evie said.

"No, she won't get it. I suppose it'll go to Melvin," Beth said. "Of course, he already has a house, so he'll probably just sell it."

"A house where someone was killed? That's a hard sell."

"Maybe. But with all the families displaced by the flood, maybe not. Anyway, Miss Archer wasn't killed there. She was killed in the hospital. As far as anyone knows, the original heart attack was natural. And it wasn't her first."

"What about Jack? Is he going to stick around for a while?"

"I think so. He's staying with his sister and helping her update the place," Beth said. "The first update has already happened. He insisted that Tillie install a phone. And I was her first phone call. She invited us for tea. I told her we probably can't make it until after finals."

"Finals are a ways off yet."

"We can go sooner if you want. Let's pick a time when we're both free, and I'll call and let her know when we can make it."

"Sounds good." Evie smiled again. "Maybe we'll hear more about Jack and Miss Archer."

"Yeah? I think I might have heard enough about that for the time being. Maybe we should close the book on this case."

"Speaking of books, did you find out if the Shakespeare books are genuine or not?"

"Yup. They are genuine, according to Miss Tanner's expert. Although they're not in tip-top shape, they're still pretty valuable. The final decision about what to do with them will be up to the library board. Miss Tanner and I are going to suggest selling them and setting up an Almira Archer Fund for the library. Our library certainly doesn't need a rare books department."

"That sounds wonderful."

"Yeah. And I'd get to manage the collection, which would be fun. Now, shall we move into the kitchen?" Beth said. "I need to check on the chicken and start some water boiling for the pasta."

Evie followed Beth into the kitchen. Chestnut opened one eye, stretched, yawned, and then curled up to finish his nap.

Made in the USA
Monee, IL
03 August 2024

63222780R00184